THE BLOND
LEADING
THE BLOND

THE BLOND
LEADING
THE BLOND

•

Jayne Ormerod

AVALON BOOKS
NEW YORK

Published by Avalon Books,
an imprint of Thomas Bouregy & Co., Inc.
160 Madison Avenue, New York, NY 10016

Library of Congress Cataloging-in-Publication Data

Ormerod, Jayne.
  The blond leading the blond / Jayne Ormerod.
        p. cm.
  ISBN 978-0-8034-7609-7 (hardcover : alk. paper)
1. Socialites—Fiction.   2. Elementary school teachers—
Fiction.   3. Socialites—Crimes against—Fiction.
4. Inheritance and succession—Fiction.   5. Ohio—
Fiction.   I. Title.
  PS3615.R575B58 2011
  813'.6—dc22

                                             2011018714

PRINTED IN THE UNITED STATES OF AMERICA
ON ACID-FREE PAPER
BY RR DONNELLEY, BLOOMSBURG, PENNSYLVANIA

*This book is dedicated to all those
who believed in me. Thank you.*

Chapter One

The hounds of hell were hot on my heels.

Well, one hound, anyway. And the small white terrier wasn't so much on my heels as it was snapping like a crocodile at the side pocket of my jacket. I had flashbacks of my fourth birthday party, at which a rottweiler had ripped my arm to shreds. Premonitions of the terrier's teeth tearing into my jugular pushed me into survival-of-the-fattest mode.

Lifting my knees to my chest, pointing my chin toward the heavens, and pumping my arms like the connecting rods on a steam locomotive, I raced around the circumference of a circle-shaped town park that appeared more often used by ice cream cone–licking tourists than a crazed woman being chased by a demonic canine.

I heard the dog's owner call from behind, "Pipsqueak Rapscallion Zucker. Come here, or no treats for you tonight."

The threats fell on deaf doggie ears.

I stumbled, now listing portside with the added weight of the mongrel attached to my bisque-pink pinstripe blazer. Brand-new, I might add, and its purchase had exhausted my seasonal clothing budget.

I swatted in the dog's general direction, my hand brushing across a cold, wet, snarling snout. Glancing down, I saw his little back paws paddling in the air as he flew behind me like an experienced parasailor. A parasailor with tiny, white, piranha-like teeth. For lack of a better plan, I turned my attention forward, my legs pumping faster as I raced along, hoping the dog would fall off before my lungs exploded from my chest. Judging

1

by the current level of pain throbbing beneath my breastbone, I'd be down in less than half a lap.

"Pippy, you're being a bad boy."

The voice seemed much closer than it had on our last trip past the gazebo. I glanced back again and, in doing so, broke the first rule of running, which also happens to be the first rule of life: *Always look where you're going.*

The next thing I knew, I was on the ground, sandwiched between one wriggling, semi-squishy body beneath me and one squirming, bony-elbowed body on top of me, with the terrier snarling and tugging at my pocket like a seagull on a discarded peanut butter sandwich. Small comfort that he wasn't the least bit interested in shredding my flesh.

I felt the weight lift off my back, and I rolled onto the grass and looked heavenward. Pippy's owner stared down at me. She was a well-seasoned citizen, judging by her tight blue curls and cheeks that had given themselves up to gravity. She was wearing three-inch platform heels, yet she'd outsprinted me. Pathetic.

"Are you okay?" she asked, while exorcising the terrier from my jacket.

Good question. I struggled to a semi-sitting position and tried to catch my breath while conducting a quick mental inventory of all my two thousand body parts. Sore knees, dirt under the fingernails, Jackie-O sunglasses askew, and an unnatural breeze along my upper thighs. I did my best wriggle-and-tug until the hem of my skirt returned to a respectable level. It's not my nature to reveal so much of myself. Especially to strangers.

And there were more strangers than I cared to count, pressing in an ever-tightening circle around me. The curiosity seekers wore identical expressions, feigning horror while concealing amusement. So much for sneaking unnoticed into and then out of the town founded by my many-generations-removed grandfather. Then again, I don't often get away with sneaking, on account of my size. I measure in at a smidgen over six feet and my weight, well, I'd stopped monitoring it when my scale kept insisting I'd crossed the two-hundred-pound mark. Now, on account of my screaming and running, it seemed as if the entire town had taken notice of my arrival. As if a band director had just lowered his baton, the whispers began. I picked up snippets of conversations.

"Could that be Ellery Tinsdale?"

"I read in the *Bugle* she was dead."

"She has the Tinsdale mouth."

"Look at those hands. I would think someone of her lineage would take more care of her appearance."

"I expected a much younger woman. She's old enough for a Golden Buckeye card."

Ouch. That hurt. I'd always looked older, and wiser, than my years. I'd purchased my first six-pack of Pabst Blue Ribbon at age twelve without even so much as a raised eyebrow from the convenience-store clerk. I'd never fought nature and wore my blond-fading-to-gray hair and curse-of-a-sun-worshipper wrinkles as a banner of honor, and I didn't expect to hear from AARP for another ten years.

"I must apologize for Pippy, here," the dog's owner said.

I leveled my gaze at the dog, held by its owner within jugular-piercing range. Pipsqueak stared at me and licked his chops. I put my hand to my neck, tucking thumb and forefinger close against my pulse points.

The woman shoved the frothing beast so that we were nose to nose. So close that I could feel his steamy breath and smell the remnants of the three-day-old carcass he'd had for lunch. Before I could recoil, his tongue snaked out and licked the tip of my nose.

A chorus of "Awwws" rippled through the crowd. Not an "awww" moment from my perspective. I scrubbed the doggie germs away with the back of my hand.

The woman tugged Pipsqueak back into the crook of her arm and patted his head. "The only time he ever acts that way is when a hamburger is involved." Her voice slid two octaves up the diatonic scale as she spoke. She twisted the dog so that they could kiss, Eskimo-style. "He wuves his hamburgers, wes he does. Wes he does." After some unintelligible doggie babble, she looked back at me and beamed like a proud momma. "He's acting as if you were wearing Eau de Big Mac perfume or something." The crowd laughed at her joke.

I didn't, but I understood the unprovoked attack. Being on a new half-diet (eating half of the usual amount of my favorite foods), I'd tucked the uneaten portion of my triple-decker bacon cheddar burger away. Crinkling the paper a few times since lunch served as a testament to my willpower. I hadn't been nearly as successful with the French fries.

Reaching into my pocket, I extracted the long-gone-cold half-burger and handed it to Pippy's owner. "He must have smelled this."

She took the proffered wad of foil and unwrapped it. Pip-squeak vibrated like a tuning fork as she did so, then wriggled free before the wrapper hit the ground. One bite and it was gone. Maybe it was a trick of the light, but I think the dog winked at me while licking ketchup and beef juice from his whiskers.

His owner beamed at me as if I'd just given her dog my last morsel of food, not my three-hour-old garbage.

"Let's break it up now, folks. Show's over." A man with a gun on his hip and a swagger to his gait began shooing away the crowd.

I'm no detective, not by any stretch of the imagination, but I suspected that the grass stains on the back of his white uniform shirt were because he was the poor soul who'd been the lowest layer of our human sandwich. I hoped assaulting a police officer while fleeing a hamburger-crazed dog wasn't a crime in Braddocks Beach, Ohio. I had no intention of spending a night in the pokey. In fact, I had no intention of spending a night in this town at all. I wanted to see the sights, which, judging by the dot on the map, shouldn't take more than ten minutes, collect my token inheritance from an aunt I'd heard of only once as a child, and be heading back home to Virginia Beach in time to pack my bags for a monthlong cruise to Alaska.

I'd been planning and saving for it for three years. My ship sailed in two weeks. Three hundred and twenty-two hours, to be exact. Not that I was counting.

The crowd backed off but didn't disperse. The chatter became more frenetic and suppositional as I hauled myself, none too gracefully, to my feet. I started brushing yard debris from my clothes. My actions stilled as I caught the police officer's eyes, mere slits in a sea of scowling flesh and a bulbous nose sticking out like a Bozo's Bop Bag. Albert Bennett, Chief of Police, according to his nameplate. "Ms. Tinsdale, I presume?" he said in an officious tone.

I stood a good six inches taller than the chief and used my height to trump his badge. I didn't like the way he'd said "Ms.," as if it left a bad taste in his mouth. "It's *Miss* Tinsdale," I said. I was proud of my single status. After more failed marriages than I cared to count, I'd vowed to remain a "Miss" for the rest of my life.

Chief Bennett's scowl tightened as he dipped his head. His hands assumed the position of authority, sliding to his belt. His left hand rested on the butt of his gun, his fingers fluttering against it as if his trigger finger had an itch. Advantage: Chief Bennett.

"*Miss* Tinsdale," he said with all the friendliness of a cornered whistle pig. "Allow me to welcome you to Braddocks Beach. I hope you'll make time in your schedule to stop by the station and have a word with us. I have a few questions I'd like to ask you with regard to your aunt's murder."

I inhaled so quickly I feared the gaggle of Canada geese waddling through the park would adopt me into their flock. But I wasn't alone in my surprise. Looking around, I realized the word *murder* was just as much a shock to the crowd as it was to me. Aunt Izzy had been murdered?

"And don't think for a minute that just because your great-great-great-great-granddaddy founded this town that you'll get any sort of special treatment."

"Huh?" I always hated it when my third-grade science

students "huh-ed" me, but it was the most intelligent thing I could think to say at that moment. What exactly was this man implying?

"You've got means," he said, sizing me up and down. "And motive. All I have to do is prove opportunity, and you'll spend the rest of your life looking through the steel bars of the Marysville Women's Reformatory. I hope you have a good alibi for the early-morning hours of May thirtieth."

"Huh?"

Chapter Two

Bennett, you have about as much subtlety as a freight train," said a woman elbowing herself through the crowd of on-lookers until she found her way to my side. While her shoulder barely reached my elbow, her mountain of platinum curls tickled my earlobe. The margarita-green pantsuit she wore was a bit hard on the eyes, not to mention a bit formal for a Friday afternoon stroll through the park.

"If you're gonna be chief of a small town, you need to park your big-city attitude at the door," she continued. "Haven't you ever heard of 'innocent until proven guilty'?"

I'm not sure she realized her French-tipped nails were digging into my forearm, but far be it from me to complain to somebody who was defending my honor. I've never even killed a spider, let alone another human being. And I'd have told the chief that myself, had the shock of learning of Aunt Izzy's murder and me being a suspect not temporarily severed my brain-to-tongue connection.

The little big-haired woman stepped forward, dragging me with her until we were toe to toe with the man with a gun. "Mayor Twiddy is going to be mighty interested to hear how you welcome new citizens to town. Especially someone of Miss Tindale's lineage." She spoke loud enough for those in the back row to hear, punctuating every other syllable with a finger poke to Chief Bennett's star badge. "Why don't you just go back to where you came from? Oh, that's right. They don't want you either." An extra hard poke knocked him a step backward. Snickers and snorts rippled through the assemblage while the chief's entire face, including his clown nose, turned an unflattering shade of merlot.

The woman seemed to have the situation well in hand. I settled as far back on my heels as her grip on me would allow, perfectly content to let her handle things.

Without missing a beat, she continued her finger-poking tirade. "I have yet to understand what Mayor Twiddy saw in you that led him to think you were the best candidate for the job, but don't think this latest incident won't be reported at the next city council meeting. Better have your bags packed, Bennett, because we're ready to run you out of town." The woman spun around to face me. A genuine smile lit her petite face. "Come with me, Miss Tinsdale." Her voice was as sweet as it could be without having a Southern drawl. "I'll show you some small-town hospitality. How does a cup of coffee and a slice of the best homemade apple pie this side of Lake Erie sound?"

I guess she took my grimace of pain as assent. She tugged me away from the crowd, which parted like the waters for Moses, and towed me along the sidewalk at a pace that would give the fillies at Belmont a run for their money.

"That's your forefather," she said, nodding as we breezed past the stern gaze of a bronze statue who, I noticed, did have my mouth.

"That's Charlie Braddock." Another statue. This one was more than double life size, and it intimidated the hell out of me.

After crossing against traffic, we marched along the sidewalk circle until we came to Reba's Pie-ery, which, based on the tantalizing aromas combined with the signage, I deduced specialized in pies. Who'd have thunk this small dot on the map would have such culinary specialties? Not me.

It wasn't until we were settled in a back booth that the woman released my arm from her death grip. My gaze flitted to my forearm, where the angry, moon-shaped imprints from her fingernails had left their mark. Thankfully, she hadn't drawn blood. Nine times out of ten, I faint at the sight of it. Ten out of ten if it's my own.

I glanced around, fighting against the mental paralysis caused by sensory overload. Red. Black. Chrome. Plastic. Simple. Serviceable. Loud. Elvis. (His long-sideburn days.) And the heavenly scent of still-bubbling-in-the-oven apple pie.

"Coffee and pie, here," the woman seated across from me shouted to a passing waitress, then turned her attention back to me. "Do you want ice cream on it?"

I hesitated, thinking about my half-diet and wondering if I'd rather limit myself to one full piece of pie without ice cream or one half of a piece with creamy vanilla melting over it.

"Be it apple or humble, pie should always be served à la mode," the woman tempted me.

Just as I was about to agree, I remembered my diet. With a firm head shake, I declined the ice cream and resolved to enjoy only half of the unembellished pie.

"My name is Samantha Greene. Born, raised, and still residing in the house next to Mizizzy." She pronounced it in one word, with the accent on the first *z*. "Your Aunt Isabel," she clarified. "Peace be with her."

We shook hands, exchanged polite bits of personal information, and agreed that I would call her Sam and she would call me Ellery. I have a bad association with the nickname Ellie, since the boys in my grade school couldn't say my nickname without preceding it with the adjective Smelly, and truncated El to me was not a name, just a letter that followed the letter *K*.

Sam focused her attention on arranging the standard-diner-issue salt and pepper shakers next to the tin napkin dispenser, giving me an opportunity to study this short, slight, and buzzing-with-energy woman who reminded me of a leprechaun. Up close, she looked older than my first impression of twentysomething. Her peaches-and-cream skin gave testimony to expensive facial creams, but small cracks indicated she hadn't succumbed to Botox. Her who-the-hell-cares-what-other-people-think-of-me aura came only after a woman's fortieth birthday. She had a twenty-thousand-watt smile, yet it was her eyes that held my attention. Bright. Emerald green. And accusing.

"Do you have an alibi for Memorial Day weekend?" she asked in that soft, but not southern, way.

"No." I'd spent the weekend nursing a summer cold and watching a *Mary Tyler Moore* marathon. "But I didn't kill my aunt, like that police chief seems to think."

"Of course you didn't." Her voice carried above the din of the kitchen to my left, where waitresses shouted orders and short-order cooks banged spatulas against stainless-steel counters. But her eyes still held me in judgment. "Tinsdales are pacifists by genetics. I've known three generations of your family and have read the complete, unabridged history on the preceding seven. Not a bad seed among them. Don't worry. We'll work something out." She removed the jelly tubs from their corral and began sorting them by flavor.

It was disconcerting the way this stranger knew more about my family than I did. But then again, since my father had never mentioned his association with Braddocks Beach, every citizen in town probably knew more about my heritage than I did, what with my ancestor's statue in the center of town and all.

Two cups of steaming, fragrant coffee slid across the table, and one stopped right under my nose. *Ah, the nectar of the gods.*

Sam pushed the sugar bowl and cream pitcher my way. "I've been waiting to meet you since your grandmother's deathbed confession that your father was alive, despite his obituary in the *Braddocks Beach Bugle* in October 1967."

"Huh?" *I really must stop doing that.*

"How much of Braddocks Beach history have you heard?"

"Only what's posted on the town's website." My cyber-research had revealed that Frederick Tinsdale had settled the area with Charles Braddock as part of the Western Reserve in 1853. A spitting contest had been held to determine who the mill town—nestled in the *V* of a heart-shaped 7,900-acre lake—would be named after. Braddock had won.

"But your father talked about it, right?"

"Nope. Never mentioned it. I found out about Braddocks

Beach when I received a letter from some attorney asking me to come here today."

Sam let out a breath that must have depleted every last molecule of carbon dioxide from her lungs, then inhaled in a way that sucked her nostrils closed. "Okay," she began, "short version—your father was a Tinsdale, by deed and action. He took his duty very seriously, worked hard in school, was actively involved in community matters, and was prepared to take over the family businesses. But on the night before the class of '58 commencement exercises, he disappeared. Not a word to his mother, not a good-bye to his baby sister—your Aunt Izzy—and forsaking his title of valedictorian, which made no sense. Crazy Martha Stinson gave the commencement address that day, to the embarrassment of the entire town. There was some talk she'd had something to do with your father's disappearance, but nothing was ever proved. Nobody ever heard from your dad again, and that's when the rumors started."

"Rumors?"

"They don't bear repeating, but suffice it to say, they were a disgrace to the Tinsdale name. I never did put much stock into them, but you know how small towns go—"

I nodded. I didn't know from personal experience, but I'd watched my share of Andy Griffith reruns.

"Nobody knows where your dad lived from '58 to '67, but in October of that year our prodigal son returned to Braddocks Beach. In a pine box. He'd dodged the draft by escaping to Canada, where he'd been killed by a bear."

"My dad never dodged the draft. He served in the navy for twenty-three years. He and mom died in an accident fifteen years ago—"

"Hold on, you're getting ahead of me here. Gertrude Irene Tinsdale, that would be your grandmother, got tired of having the Tinsdale name dragged through the mud, so she invented the story of your father's death, paid for a full-page obituary in the paper, held a proper funeral—trust me, there wasn't a dry eye in the house—and had him interred in the family crypt. At that point, your family, and the town, put a period to that chapter of Braddocks Beach history. Your grand-mother spun a story of his 'lost' "—Sam put air quotes around the word—"years in Canada. Even wrote a book about them. Only on her deathbed, a few months ago, Miss Gert confessed to her lie. For all Mizizzy knew, Jack was alive and well. Turns out, he wasn't, but he'd lived until 1990. I'm sorry for your loss, by the way. But a week before Mizizzy's death, her search found you, the last surviving member of the Tinsdale legacy. I guess you've changed your name a lot?"

I nodded. For almost forty years, I'd held a romanticized no-tion of wedded bliss, and had walked down the aisle with who-ever proposed, in hopes that I'd found my forever-and-ever-Amen man. Reality often hit within a few weeks. One lasted almost eighteen months. Last year I swore off marriage for good and reverted back to my maiden name. I felt no compunction to share the etymology of my name with Sam, despite the preg-nant silence hanging between us.

Sam sighed and continued from where she'd left off. "The day the detective called to say he'd found you, Mizizzy screamed so loud one of the neighbors called the police. Too bad your aunt died—I mean was killed—before you two could meet." Sam tapped her spoon against her mug and set it on the For-mica without making the slightest sound. "You're the closest thing we have to royalty. I hope you're prepared."

"Prepared? For what?" I asked with all the enthusiasm of someone who had just been informed her car's transmission needed work and was waiting to hear how much it would cost.

"To take up Mizizzy's role as Queen Bee, of course."

"What's a Queen Bee?" I asked even more hesitantly.

"An honor is bestowed upon you based on heredity. The Braddock lineage died out over a hundred years ago, so the Tinsdales have been wearing the imperial tiara—diamond encrusted, I might add—ever since. You'll make appearances, lead charity drives, head up committees, set fashion trends, and such."

I didn't like the sound of it. Not one bit. And if it involved white gloves and party manners, I was doomed. To this day,

I held the honor of being the only young lady to flunk out of Madame Rowena's School of Etiquette, and she'd been in business for over sixty years.

"You timed your arrival perfectly," Sam continued. "The summer social season is just ramping up. I expect invitations are already being stuffed through your mail slot."

Two pieces of three-inch-thick pie arrived at our table. My piece absorbed 90 percent of my attention, leaving a scant 10 percent attuned to Sam's continuing diatribe on all things societal.

"We'll weed through them and select only those worthy of your appearance."

Cinnamon-scented steam curled from the slits in the crust, and I had to lick the saliva oozing out my lips.

"The Historical Society will be meeting Wednesday night to discuss the details of writing up your personal history to add to the town's register. Inquiring minds will want to know all about you."

Not taking my gaze off what can best be described as the Fourth Wonder of the Dessert World, my hands fumbled to remove the paper band holding the paper napkin around my utensils.

"Holy Carpe Diem. Look at the time."

I looked up and at Sam and then back down. My pie was gone. Sam had pushed my plate to the edge of the table as if sending a message to the waitress that we were finished. I had not yet begun to eat.

"You've got to be at Max's office in three minutes for the reading of the will." Sam was out of her seat and pulling me out of mine.

"But my pie—" Even I winced at the whiny note that had crept into my voice.

"Forget the pie. You can't miss your appointment with Max. He's a very busy man." Once she got me standing, she maneuvered herself behind me and pushed me toward the door. The little leprechaun woman had amazing strength and fortitude.

Once we reached the sidewalk, Sam spun me to my left and

pointed. "Max's office is the seventh door down, between Mason's Tack and Saddlery and Granny Annie's Antiques and Collectables. Can't miss it. Go up the flight of stairs—they're more substantial than they look—and Max's office is on your left. He's a stickler for promptness, so you'd better get a move on. You don't want to get on his bad side, because we're going to need his help."

"Help doing what?"

"Why, finding Mizizzy's killer, of course. You don't expect that bumbling Bennett to do it, do you? That man couldn't find a polar bear in a field of buttercups. And it sounds as if he's already got you tried and convicted. You'll need to do this yourself. You're a Tinsdale, after all. Duty and honor to the name. You owe it to your aunt. And your father. Max can help. Hurry now. I'll catch up with you later at Mizizzy's house. Max will give you the key. I'll prepare a bedroom for you." She gave me a powerful shove to get me going.

One time, many years ago, I'd been tricked into riding the Tilt-A-Whirl at the county fair. It had spun in circles while revolving around on a tilted platform. When it stopped after what had seemed like an eternity, I was so dizzy I fell down twice trying to get back onto solid ground. The feeling lasted for nine days.

Right now, I felt like I had when the ride had just been warming up. I knew what was going to happen, and I wanted to get off before I became too dizzy to walk, but I wasn't sure whom to yell at to stop this Tilt-A-Whirl of life.

Chapter Three

Geoffrey Maxamillion Eddington III, Esquire, the man who'd requested my presence at today's reading of Isabel Tinsdale's will, did not live up to his grand name. I'd had a preconceived notion of a man with a sophisticated air and a full head of thick salt-and-pepper hair. Max, as he insisted I call him, was but a babe in the woods, a few shades this side of scrawny, and appeared to be bald by choice, not genetics. He acted as twitchy as a gerbil in a room full of hungry tomcats as he peered at me over the top of a pair of half-glasses, the likes of which you grab on impulse at the Big-Mart checkout aisle. His double-buttoned charcoal suit was impeccable and still had the manufacturer's label tacked to the sleeve. Purchased on my behalf? It seemed fitting, since my outfit had been purchased on his.

A highly polished oak desk separated us as we sat waiting for another beneficiary to join us. I glanced around the room at the office's décor, straight out of a Legal-Offices-R-Us catalog, which included walls lined with a leather-bound collection of Ohio legal codes and color-coordinated tan leather furniture. The room had the aroma of money. Old money. Lots and lots of very old money. Not in the physical sense, per se, but in the metaphorical one. The only oddity was the piece of artwork hanging on the wall directly behind Max, a tapestry of Coolidge's *Dogs Playing Poker*. One point to Max for his sense of humor, and another for not engaging me in senseless small talk. I was not in a chatty mood.

The office door clicked open, and I swiveled my head to see Merry Sue, Max's secretary whom I'd met on my way in,

15

standing in the doorway. "Mr. Littleton is here," she announced in a soft, sexy voice that belied her Marian the Librarian appearance.

Max jumped from his chair and scurried around his desk toward the door. "Connie. Haven't seen you since the funeral."

I rose from my chair and turned to face the newcomer.

"Thank you, Max." While the two shook hands and squeezed shoulders, the stranger's eyes remained focused on me. "And you must be Ellery."

At my height, it wasn't often I looked up to anyone, but Connie Littleton had a good three inches on me, much like my father. And also like him, Connie had eyes that twinkled like Santa Claus, surrounded by lines that gave testament to a life of laughter. Sporting a crisp white buttoned-down shirt that matched the color of his wavy hair, well-worn (and possibly ironed) Levis, and dusty cowboy boots, he had an aura of sophistication that outclassed Max's new suit.

I smiled as Mr. Littleton stepped toward me and accepted my proffered hand with his right and then capped it off with his left. Strong hands accustomed to hard work.

"I'm Conrad Littleton," he said. "I had great respect for your aunt. Please accept my condolences. Her time on earth was much too short."

"Thank you, Mr. Littleton."

"Connie, please." He smiled and gave my hand a gentle squeeze before releasing it. "I see you have the Tinsdale mouth. And the Spires chin. Your aunt would have been tickled with that."

Max cleared his throat. "If you would both be seated, we'll begin. Coffee anyone? I can have Merry Sue—"

"None for me, thank you," Connie said.

"Me either." I settled in the short-backed side chair Connie held for me. He dragged its twin close and sat. We both turned to Max, waiting for him to begin.

Max's paper shuffling and pen collecting echoed in the silence. His obvious attempt to stall gave me too much time to think.

What had been in the dark and scary recesses of my mind now held the spotlight dance. In a few minutes, I would inherit something that would connect me to ancestors I hadn't known existed until last week. A small piece of jewelry worn by my great-grandmother or a tie clip used by my father in his youth would mean more to me than all the money in the world. I'd have a connection to my ancestors. I'd have a sense of who my father was. And I'd have a better understanding of myself. That could as easily be a bad thing as a good thing. I shivered off the dark thoughts and focused on the bright ones.

"Let's begin, then." Max slid two folders across the table, one each for Connie and myself.

My thighs flapped together until I stilled them with a vise-like grip just above the knees. A glance at Connie showed him to be sitting straight-backed and still. He obviously didn't have as much at stake here.

"These are complete copies for you to take with you. I'll file it for probate later this week, but as you'll see, there are some conditions to be met before all the funds can be disbursed."

Max cleared his throat and began reading the legalese, proclaiming Isabel Genevieve Tinsdale to be of sound mind and body when she'd prepared the document two days before her death. First on the list of beneficiaries was the Historical Society. Max flipped to the next page and continued. "The Braddocks Beach Church of Divine Spiritual Enlightenment will be given five hundred thousand dollars, for the construction of a community room. It will be named the Tinsdale Room." Max stopped reading and peered over the glasses and his paper at me. "Your aunt was greatly concerned that your family name would disappear from local history, not being at all sure what your desires would be."

I nodded my understanding. Sort of. The concept of any building sharing my name was foreign. And very disturbing. It's a good thing Virginia Beach is six hundred miles away, and I could continue my life in relative anonymity.

Max rambled on about significant sums going to the American Cancer Society, the American Heart Association, the

American Lung Association, the National Endowment for the Performing Arts, the National Association for Adoption Search and Reunion, the Cleveland Orchestra and its chorus, the high school performing arts department, the local SPCA, Boy Scouts, Girl Scouts, the local chapter of the Red Hat Society, and on and on and on. So much money. Already well into the millions, if my math was accurate. To say Aunt Izzy had been loaded was an understatement. How had she escaped the Forbes list for so many years?

I stopped listening and thought about a woman who was so magnanimous. I liked her. Could probably learn a lot from her. Could have—past tense—I reminded myself. My grip on my knees tightened.

"To my dear friend and confidant," Max read on, "Conrad Avery Littleton, I leave the sum of two hundred and fifty thousand dollars for the purposes of pursuing the project we were working on. He is aware of this bequest and will know what my wishes are in this regard."

Connie started squirming in his seat. I started squirming, too, and pulled at a thread of the floral appliqué on the lapel of my jacket, picked some of Pipsqueak's white fur from my skirt, and tapped my toes against the carpet.

"Ellery."

Hearing Max say my name, I turned my attention to him. My fidgeting came to a screeching stop. My nerves felt as taut as piano strings. The ones in the top-seventh octave range.

"I leave all remaining property to my niece, Ellery Elizabeth Tinsdale. The condition of this bequest is that she must reside within the city limits of Braddocks Beach, taking up residence in the house on Charleston Street where generations of Tinsdales have lived, for five years."

I stared at Max, who shuffled the papers as if he hadn't just pushed the button to launch the Tomahawk missile into my life. Me? Live in this two-statue town? For five years? I'd die of suffocation before the next Memorial Day parade. That's if the snow didn't kill me first. I hate cold weather.

"And that's about it," he said. "There are more specific

instructions on the distribution of assets should you not meet your residency requirements, but you can read that yourself." He nodded at the file in front of me.

Complete silence settled around us as I digested this information. I felt Connie's and Max's eyes upon me. Drawing forth the mental scales, I weighed my duty to the family name against the duty to myself to continue my work molding young minds. After all those charitable bequests, there couldn't be much money left for me. I'd cherish some token of my father's family—a pocket watch, a family photo album. But a little bit of money might convince me to stay. Enough that I could fulfill my dream of a summerlong cruise from Alaska to Chile. "How much are we talking about?" I asked.

"Miss Izzy had vast real estate holdings within the community, as well as a sizable investment portfolio sufficiently diversified to balance risks. With the bull market of late, it's very healthy. All told, I'm guessing the entire estate is well into the eight digits."

I closed my eyes and started counting zeros while pressing my fingers as numeric placeholders into the leather armrest. One, tens, hundreds, thousands, ten thousands, hundred thousands, millions—

The Tilt-A-Whirl started spinning faster.

A one and seven zeros was in the ten millions. And Max had implied well into. I checked, double-checked, then triple-checked my finger-tapping math. The amount was staggering. Mind-boggling. Utterly incomprehensible to a woman who made forty-six thousand per year and managed to spend every single penny of it.

To put it mildly, it scared the bejesus out of me.

Max's voice penetrated my thoughts. "Miss Tinsdale, are you okay?" quickly followed by, "I think she's in shock."

That's all I remember before my world faded to black.

Chapter Four

The first, and only, thing I noticed when I let myself in the back door to Aunt Izzy's house was a white, pie-shaped Styrofoam container with TAKE A PIECE OF REBA HOME emblazoned in folksy red letters on the lid. I flipped it open. My mouth watered as the aroma of cinnamon, nutmeg, and apples filled the air. The delectable food I hadn't had time to eat before rushing off to meet Max. Sam could end up being a kindred spirit if she inherently understood my mind-body-food connection.

Luck was with me, as I found silverware in the first drawer I opened. I grabbed a fork and settled myself at a walnut drop-leaf kitchen table, giving little thought to the way it was set with one blue-and-white-checkered place mat, as if waiting for Aunt Izzy to come downstairs for her morning coffee and Cheerios.

I forked the first flaky bite of Reba's pie into my mouth. I had the second bite loaded and suspended in midair before I'd swallowed the first. I couldn't think on an empty stomach, and I had a lot to think about right now.

The walk through town had left me feeling confused, as if the citizens had marched boldly into the twenty-first century but the Victorian atmosphere had refused to comply. SUVs looked out of place. Horses should be standing at hitching posts in front of the old, weathered hardware store. Children's laughter filled the air, but the children surprised me when they raced around a corner on Rollerblades when I'd expected to see knickers-wearing boys using a stick to guide rolling wooden hoops along the sidewalk. Short-shorts replaced petticoats and skirts. Visors substituted for parasols. Souvenir stores stood in for dry goods shops. It was a right-place, wrong-century feeling that made me wonder if this was all a dream.

The confusion was augmented by the weak feeling generated by the fainting episode. Connie and Max had been very gracious as they'd hauled me up off the floor. For the second time in less than two hours, my skirt had been pushed to an indecent level up my thighs. I worried that if I didn't stop flaunting my assets, I would soon be labeled a Braddocks Beach hoochie momma. Not at all in keeping with whatever title Sam had given the role she expected me to play.

I focused on eating the pie, because it was just too scary to even consider the ramifications of Aunt Izzy's will. I recalled a scene in *Gone with the Wind* when Scarlett had said, "Well, I guess I've done murder. I won't think about that now. I'll think about that tomorrow." If it worked for the most famous of Southern belles, it would work for me. At least I hadn't "done murder." Convincing Chief Bennett of that was another thing I didn't want to think about at the moment.

I sighed as another bite of pie melted in my mouth. Heavenly.

The back door banged open, and Sam rushed in with the energy force of the Tasmanian devil. "How'd you get here?" she asked, her gaze focused out the small window over the kitchen sink. "I don't see your car."

"I walked."

"Is your car broken? I can have Titus over at the garage go take a look at it." She whipped a cell phone out of the pocket of her pantsuit and began punching numbers.

"No, the car's fine. I needed some exercise." I didn't want to tell her I'd been too shaky to drive. In fact, I'd been too shaky to listen to the specifics of my residency here as detailed in the will. I'd excused myself, making an appointment through Merry Sue for ten o'clock the next morning, when I hoped my mental faculties could deal with the humongous life changes. I then inquired how to find Aunt Izzy's house. Merry Sue handed me the keys, and I'd escaped out into the sunshine.

"Would it be easier for Titus to come get the key or tow your truck back here?"

I supposed the easiest thing to do would be for me to walk back up there and drive it home. It was only three blocks, but I didn't feel up to it at this point.

I listened with one ear while Sam made the decision for me. "Titus, dear, I need a favor. Miss Tinsdale is here at Mizizzy's house and her car is up at Max's office, and she'll need her suitcases and things, and she just can't get away right now. We have a backyard potluck in less than two hours, so could you hook it and haul it back for her, please? That would save time. Yes. It's the brick-red Freelander. It's a baby Land Rover. Virginia license plate B-C-H-T-C-H-R. No, I think it means Beach Teacher. Thanks so much." After a string of ums and okays, she flipped the phone shut.

I probably should have been frightened that Sam knew so much about my truck—and me—but it was nice to have the minor details arranged on my behalf. Having a car towed a half a mile as a matter of convenience seemed decidedly wasteful, but it saved me the walk all the way back up to town at the point in the day when my get-up-and-go had got up and run screaming for the hills.

"Titus is a dear man. He'll have it here in two shakes."

"Thank you," I said, hoping Bessie—the name I'd given my bold and brassy Freelander—wouldn't be too offended when given "the hook." She'd become quite temperamental in her old age. If she were a horse, she'd have been sent to the glue factory years ago. As it was, she had one wheel in the junkyard.

Sam tugged the chrome lever handle of a short, puffy refrigerator, the likes of which I'd seen only in an antiques store. She stuck her head inside and reemerged holding a can of soda triumphantly over her head. Heel kicking the door shut, she popped open the diet cola and settled in a chair across the table from me. "Who's our prime suspect?"

"Huh?"

"You know, in your aunt's murder. I've decided you'll need help in solving this, so I'm offering my services. As any good detective knows, the beneficiaries of the will are always the prime suspects. Trust me. I read a lot of whodunits. Ninety percent of the time, it's one of the beneficiaries going for the money. Greed is the number one motive for killing another human being. So, who've we got?"

"Here's the thing, Sam." I wriggled in my seat and sat up a bit straighter, a better posture for pie digestion. "I don't think I have what it takes to track down a killer. My mom made me read all the Nancy Drews when I was a girl, and I was most sympathetic to Bess Marvin. I wished Nancy would stay home and host luncheons. Feel free to do what you feel necessary, though."

"Don't be silly, El. It's not like we're going to end up in a shootout at an abandoned warehouse or anything. We're talking Braddocks Beach, not New York City. We'll talk, look, and listen. I'm friends with everyone here, and they'll talk to me where they won't talk to the police. As beneficiary, you'll have access to death certificates and other documents that might give us a clue. Then we'll sit here in Mizizzy's safe little kitchen, put all the puzzle pieces together, and turn it over to the police—not Bennett, but another officer—for capture. Trust me, no danger whatsoever."

I still wasn't convinced I wanted to participate, but Sam did not seem to be in an arguing mood. I'd humor her, for now. "Where do we start?"

"With the beneficiaries of the will. Who are they?"

"Me, mostly." In five years, I added mentally, but it didn't seem that pesky detail was any of Sam's business.

"I figured. But we've already established you didn't do it."

Bless her for believing in me.

"Who else?" She took a dainty sip of her diet cola, pinky finger extended as if she were drinking out of one of the Queen of England's china teacups.

I took a healthy slurp of my cold soda and tried to recall names on the long list of those who had inherited money. I'd left my copy of the will on Max's desk. "The big national charities, heart, cancer, et cetera. Locally, the Red Hat Society, the scouts, the church, and Connie Littleton."

I wasn't the least bit fazed when soda shot from Sam's nose.

That was a daily occurrence in the elementary school lunch-room. Judging by the mortified look on Sam's face, it was not acceptable in the polite society of Braddocks Beach. I grabbed a napkin from the holder on the center of the table and passed it to her, then turned my attention to finishing my pie, giving her opportunity to regain her composure, which, to her credit, she accomplished quickly.

"Connie doesn't need money. His income's been curtailed since his car accident five years ago left him with back pain that prevents him from working full time, but he's far from a charity case," she said, dabbing puddles of soda from the table.

"The money's not for him, but for some secret project the two were working on."

"How much?"

"Quarter of a million. He got squirmy when Max mentioned it."

"Connie wouldn't kill anyone."

"I didn't mean to imply that," I said, stretching the truth. I mean, I didn't *seriously* think Connie had killed Aunt Izzy, because he just looked too kindhearted and gentle, but now that I thought about it, his fidgetiness had been that of someone guilty of something. "But maybe whatever secret project he and Aunt Izzy had could give someone motive for murder."

"Oh, now that's interesting." Sam stared at the ceiling, as if contemplating the meaning of life.

The deepest thought I was having had to do with how to get the last few pie crumbs from the Styrofoam container to my mouth. Were I alone, I'd have no compunction about dragging my tongue across the surface the way a cat laps up the last drops of milk from a saucer. I do remember Madame Rowena frowning at that behavior, so I settled for crunching the crumbs in the tines of the fork, then dragging it across my outstretched tongue like it was an ice cream cone.

"I can call Reba's and have another piece delivered if you're still hungry."

I jumped, not realizing Sam had been watching me. "No,

thanks. Just wanted to make sure the fork was clean before I put it back in the drawer."

A look of pure, unadulterated horror passed over Sam's face.

"I'm kidding. I'll put it in the dishwasher."

"Mizizzy doesn't have a dishwasher." Sam hopped up from her chair, took the utensil from my hand, and cleared the Styrofoam from in front of me. I heard the water running and swiveled my head to see her washing the fork with dish soap and steamy water.

I contemplated life without a dishwasher and shivered. I enjoyed reading about Laura Ingalls Wilder and her life as pioneer girl, but I had no desire to live that way. I predicted plastic cutlery and paper plates in my future. If I stayed. And while the money sure weighted heavily in that direction, I'd be giving up absolutely everything that defined me. Five years seems like forever. Especially without a dishwasher.

"Did Max happen to mention the official cause of Mizizzy's death?" Sam interrupted my thoughts.

"Nope." My gaze drifted to a framed front page from the *Cleveland Plain Dealer* hanging on the wall. Above the fold was a three-column-wide photo of a tall, thin, elderly woman standing on the front porch of this house, holding a large trophy over her head. Isabel Tinsdale. I knew that as certainly as I knew my own name. "Tell me what you know about how she died."

"Her body was found at the bottom of the steps of the watchtower by an early-morning beach jogger on May thirtieth."

Even though I hadn't given it any thought up until this moment, I felt relief she hadn't died in this house. I didn't believe in ghosts, but I didn't *not* believe in them either. And didn't want to test my premise by sharing the space with the soul of a brutally murdered woman. "What and where is the watchtower?" I hoped it wasn't so close the ghost could wander home.

Sam busied herself with scrubbing the counter. "The watchtower's on the beach, catty-corner from here. Built in the early nineteen hundreds, it's modeled after one on Cape Cod. I'm not sure what its original purpose was, but now it's used by tourists for a great view over the lake, especially in the fall, when the leaves are at their peak color. On a clear summer day, it feels like you can reach out and touch a cloud. Of course, teenagers have used it as a secret rendezvous for as long as I can remember."

At the rate Sam was scrubbing, I was going to have the cleanest countertop in all of Ohio.

"According to the Tri-B, that's the *Braddocks Beach Bugle,* our weekly newspaper, Mizizzy's cause of death was accidental. If she'd fallen down the steps, which is current conjecture, Julian Potter over at Potters Funeral Home would have been able to cover up a head bruise or rebuild a collapsed nose, and it would have been an open-casket event. He is known throughout the state as a cadaver *ar-teest.*" She dragged out the last syllable. "Her death had to have been so disfiguring Julian couldn't make her look presentable. Now that we know it's murder, I'm convinced it had to be a gun. Up close and personal. Blew her face completely away—" Sam's scrubbing elevated to frenetic. "The area was hosed down as soon as the body was removed. No yellow crime-scene tape ever appeared, because the police didn't consider it a crime. And having the watchtower closed would be bad for tourist business, of course. I don't know any more than that."

I swallowed back the apple pie rolling like a fiery ball in my stomach. I don't do gruesome well. Not since I'd seen a movie where a sheet of glass slid off the back of a truck and decapitated the person standing behind it. All in full-screen, Technicolor surround sound. I'd tossed my popcorn right there at my seat. To this day, I get a queasy feeling whenever I think about anything even remotely ghastly. Looking at the kind face of the woman in the picture and imagining her brains splattered all over the walls of a watchtower was almost more than I could handle. I pressed my cold hands to my hot cheeks.

Sam slipped back into her chair and tossed back a swig of soda as if it were a shot of rotgut whiskey, then dabbed her mouth with the corner of a paper napkin. "So there were, what, twenty or so witnesses to Chief Bennett's accusations this afternoon? Wait." Sam snapped her fingers. "One of them was Henrietta Zucker. You saw her. She's Pipsqueak's owner. There's a joke in town that the three fastest forms of communication are telegraph, telephone, and tell-a-Zucker. She makes text messaging look like the Pony Express. I can guarantee you that within ten seconds, the fact that Mizizzy was murdered was all over town. It will be on the tips of everyone's tongues tonight."

Sam tapped her nails on the table as if she were playing a Mozart sonata. "Everyone from a four-block area has been invited, and someone had to have heard or seen something that will help get our investigation off the ground. We'll ask around."

"What exactly is going on tonight?"

"Your official introduction to Braddocks Beach society. Max mentioned your arrival to me only yesterday, so I didn't have much time to throw it all together. It's a simple potluck in my backyard. I hope that's okay."

"Sure." Except for the party part. I'm not exactly a social butterfly. I'm more of a social hermit crab. Before I could voice those concerns, the sound of gears grinding screeched through the screen door.

"That must be Titus' truck outside. You have just enough time to get changed for the party."

I looked down at my pinstripe jacket with black and brown embroidery, now speckled with a few flakes of pie, a chocolate-mousse camisole, and the black stretch-denim pencil skirt that had been giving me trouble all day. "Is this too dressy?"

Sam gasped. "But you've already been seen in it today. Surely you have something else?"

I conducted a mental inventory of the clothes in my back-pack. A VIRGINIA IS FOR LOVERS T-shirt and a ketchup-stained pair of white shorts I'd worn yesterday. I'd planned to wash the shorts out tonight in the bathroom sink. The only clean shirt I had was one decorated with pastel-colored handprints of some of my students, who had been six years old at the time but were now in college. It was faded with years of washing and wearing—good enough for a ten-hour car trip, but probably not considered suitable potluck attire, let alone a societal introduction, by any stretch of the imagination. "This is it."

Sam's French-tipped nails got to tapping out a tarantella, and I swear I saw wisps of steam curling from her ears. "I'll make a call and have something delivered. Chiquita is our local fashionista and owns a small shop on the circle. I'm hoping she'll have something suitable." Sam raised her eyes heavenward and mumbled something under her breath that sounded like "Why me? Why me?" After a quick nod of farewell, she buzzed out the door like a pollen-drunk bumblebee.

I struggled from my chair and followed Sam outside, offering up a question of my own. "Why me?"

No answers were immediately forthcoming.

Chapter Five

I'd never met a karaoke machine I didn't want to bash with a baseball bat. When I heard the first warbling notes of a Patsy-Cline-wannabe's "Crazy" drifting over the lilac hedge that separated Aunt Izzy's backyard from Sam's, I had to refrain from searching for a Louisville Slugger. My already sour mood turned a tad more vinegary.

I'm not much of a small-talker, so as a general rule, I avoided parties. I steadfastly refused to attend any social function where I didn't have at least a nodding acquaintance with half the attendees. And anything that put me in the spotlight just didn't happen. Ever. Not even if it involved a hundred Clydesdales dragging me. Yet tonight, on the other side of the hedge, awaited at least a hundred people (judging by the parade of covered-dish-carrying people I'd watched from an upstairs bedroom window as they filed down Sam's driveway), of whom ninety-nine would be total strangers. And I was to be introduced as the reigning Queen Bee. Tonight's potluck would be the trifecta of despised social situations. But I couldn't very well not go, could I?

No, I couldn't. Because my little voice, no doubt influenced by the wall of pictures of Aunt Izzy in the spotlight, told me in no uncertain terms that I must make an appearance.

With my hand on the screen door, I paused to make one last check of my outfit. Sam and Chiquita had come through; a deep-purple chenille dress had been delivered to Aunt Izzy's front door, complete with black leather open-toed pumps, panty hose, shell clip-on earrings, and foundation undergarments with enough fortitude to hold my flesh firmly in place while

29

still enabling me to breathe. It earned my vote as the eighth wonder of the modern world.

With one deep breath that spread its calming effect all the way to my toes, I followed the off-key tones through the lilac hedge to Sam's backyard. I hadn't so much as put one toe across the property line before I heard Sam's voice.

"Yoo-hoo! Ellery. Over here."

A smattering of applause broke out as I stood there feeling overwhelmed—until I realized they were applauding for the karaoke singer, not me. Sweat trickled down the inside of my arm as fight-or-flight instincts warred within me. Flight had just about won out when long fingernails pressed into my lower arm, pulling me into—rather than away from—the crowd.

"You look fabulous," Sam whispered.

"Thank you." Sam looked fabulous, too, in a formfitting, backless, black-with-white-polka-dots sundress. Size zero, I figured. As were most of the other women in attendance.

"I'll introduce you around," Sam said. "The buffet will begin in about an hour. I've always felt food is a common denominator and breaks down all barriers. Who doesn't love to eat?" Sam weaved around the checkerboard-covered tables and across the yard. I followed in her wake. We stopped at a long picnic table at the foot of the deck-cum-karaoke stage. Citronella smoke curled from three tin pails spaced along the surface. Two beer bottles, one half-empty plastic margarita glass, and a butter-yellow cardigan sweater served as placeholders for guests who, I assumed, were off mingling. I felt a presence behind me. When I turned, I found myself nose-to-nose with a man the size of a bear and covered with the hair of a mountain lion.

I took one step backward.

He took three steps toward me, grinning like the proverbial cat who'd eaten a canary. He reached his beefy arms out and wrapped them around my waist, lifting me in a hug. My toes scraped against the grass as the bear/man swung me back and forth. My back snapped, crackled, and popped like a bowl of

Rice Krispies in milk. Breathing was not an option. Eventually my feet settled back on solid ground as the man held me at arm's length.

"George," Sam said. "I'd like you to meet Ellery Tinsdale. Ellery, this is my husband, George Greene."

"I swear to gawd, girl, it's good to finally meet you." His voice was as gruff as his appearance. "Your daddy was a great guy. Even though he was five years older 'n me, he always let me tag along fishing with him."

I'd come to Braddocks Beach because Aunt Izzy had died. It hadn't occurred to me I'd be facing two ghosts—hers and my dad's. He'd never talked about his childhood, and I'd never asked.

"Boy, Sammy tweren't lying when she said you've got the Tinsdale smile."

The karaoke machine squeaked to life. I recognized the music but not the words of "Tomorrow" as it blared from a speaker less than two feet from my ear. It was painful, in more ways than one, and conversation became impossible. Sam tried to yell over the music to introduce me to the rest of our table-mates who had drifted back, but we all just ended up shaking hands and nodding.

"I've had about enough of being reminded 'The sun'll come out tomorrow,' so let's take that microphone away from Zanna Wilson. She's the town treasurer. I'll introduce you, and you can give a short speech." She turned and headed toward the stage.

"No." My voice carried above the karaoke.

Sam stopped and turned around. "No speeches?"

"No. I don't do public speaking." A very embarrassing event in third grade had scarred me for life. I'd repressed the details, but not the grab-you-by-the-throat-and-suffocate-the-life-out-of-you feeling of fear that I experienced at the mere thought of speaking into a microphone.

Sam did a decent job at hiding her disappointment with a slight downturn of her lips before pasting on a bright smile.

"That's okay. I respect that. We'll just do this the old-fashioned way, then." She reached out and motioned over a thirty-something couple walking by. They were dressed in what can best be described as yacht-club casual, and the woman had a scarf tied in a way that hid her chemo-induced baldness. "Bill and Gloria Stevens, I'd like you to meet Ellery Tinsdale."

And so the next hour went. The faces of Braddocks Beach movers and shakers swam before my eyes in a dizzying kaleidoscope. As we worked the crowd, Sam tsk-tsked over the horrifying circumstances surrounding Mizizzy's death and ever so innocently inquired who they thought could have committed such a heinous act. It seems every question Nancy Drew asked garnered her a clue. *We* ended up with nothing. Zip. Zero. Zilch.

"Have I met every citizen of Braddocks Beach yet?" I asked Sam during a brief respite between introductions, affecting a yawn to resume the blood flow to my aching cheeks. My so-happy-to-meet-you smile muscles were out of shape.

Sam laughed. "We have all summer to introduce you to the rest of the town."

I'd stopped counting at thirty-seven people but had despaired of remembering even one name after the third. I didn't have my notepad with me, which meant I didn't have a snowball's chance on a southeastern Virginia's August day of remembering anyone were I to pass them on the street. I sure hoped there wasn't going to be a test.

Sam left me talking with the town's mayor, Owen Twiddle Stone, or Mayor Twiddy as he insisted I call him. He was the kind of slick-talking, hand-kissing, smarmy-smiling guy who gave politicians a bad name. To his credit, he seemed to be popular with his constituents. Despite my protests, we had a "date" arranged for eleven o'clock the following morning so that he could give me a key to the city and a tour of the historical landmarks honoring my relatives.

When Sam announced, "Dinner is served," I was the first to belly up—as much from gnawing hunger (social anxiety revs up my appetite) as to get away from Mayor Twiddy. Sam met me at the head of a string of four white-linen-covered tables overflowing with food unlike any spread I'd ever seen. The staff at my school was infamous for the potlucks of flash-frozen gourmet foodstuffs such as reheated Stouffer's lasagna and volume-discount-club thaw-and-eat finger foods. By comparison, tonight was a feast of homemade specialties that would turn my teacher friends chartreuse with envy. Everything from pulled pork barbecue to sushi filled the table. Chicken tarragon casserole, salmon mousse, chilled spaghetti and capers dressed with olive oil, and corn grilled in its husks and dripping with basil butter dotted the first table alone. I took a sampling of everything. Even though I limited myself to half-a-serving-spoon full, on account of my diet, my Chinette platter threatened to collapse under the weight of so much food.

"Queen Bees should be able to see white space on their plate." Sam's etiquette lesson was delivered with an encouraging smile, which threw me enough off balance to withhold my retort of *I was taught it's polite to take a no-thank-you helping of everything.* There were some lessons from Madame Rowena that did stick with me throughout my life.

The karaoke machine took a break while a dj played an eclectic selection of classical music. I was joined at the table by Sam's husband, George. A few moments later, Doodles Rogers, introduced as my neighbor across the street, joined us. Were I required to describe him in one adjective, it would be round—round body, round fingers, round face, round glasses.

We ate. We talked. We laughed. A lot. Sam only had to coach me one more time on my manners. "Corn should be eaten left to right, like a typewriter," she'd whispered in my ear when racing off to greet some late-arriving guests. Who'd have thunk? She buzzed back to our table and, with her once again seated across from me, I didn't dare lick the basil butter from my fingers. "If you'll excuse me for a minute." I climbed out from under the picnic table. My dinner companions nodded. George and Doodles stood up when I did—after I felt Sam kick George under the table, that is. I was glad I wasn't the only one who needed prompting when it came to all things mannerly.

Not wanting to have to shake someone's hand with my buttery fingers, I skirted around the perimeter of the party toward Sam's back door. The route took me through the shadows of a detached garage that I suspected had originally served as a carriage house. As had happened earlier that afternoon, a right-place/wrong-time-period feeling washed over me and left me thinking I'd fallen into some kind of parallel-universe time warp. I pressed my nose against the barn-style doors and inhaled deeply, expecting the scent of hay and horses to fill my nostrils. Nope. Only gasoline and decomposing lawn clippings, confirming I was still in the twenty-first century, but a long, long way from home.

I shook my head and went to step back when a strong hand wrapped around my elbow and pulled me toward the darkness behind the garage. Kick first and ask questions later had always been my motto when attacked, and my leg flew forward of its own accord. My opened-toed shoe made contact with the corner of the garage. Pain shot up my foot and leg, the likes of which I hadn't experienced since the twenty-pound-bowling-ball incident of 1987.

"Are you okay?"

I looked up and as my eyes adjusted to the dim light, I recognized Connie. His look of concern eased my pain by maybe a decibel, or whatever scale is used to register pain. I plastered a smile on my face, feeling foolish for overreacting. "Guess so many years in the big city have me afraid of my own shadow." I rubbed my toe along the back of my other leg, but the throbbing was not easily assuaged.

"I'm sorry. I didn't mean to scare you, but you looked like you were going to faint again."

"Oh, no." I dismissed his concern with a wave of my hand, hoping I wouldn't be forced to reveal the reason I'd felt compelled to sniff the door. "In fact, I feel better than I have in a long time. Something about this small-town air, I guess." It's hard to carry on a friendly conversation while your lungs want to scream out with pain and agony.

He smiled at me, which seemed to take a great deal of effort.

"Are *you* okay?" I asked, studying his ashen complexion in the sliver of moonlight. He wore the same jeans and boots as this afternoon but had added a thick, dappled sweater, despite the temperate evening air.

"I feel tired tonight," he said and sighed. "I think Izzy's death is finally hitting me, along with the realization that you've gone your entire life knowing so little of your family. Every generation of Tinsdales for a hundred and fifty years has played an important role in this town's history. Izzy anticipated the day she would bring you here and share that heritage with you. But now she's gone." He paused to clear his voice. "Would tomorrow afternoon be convenient for me to stop by?" He leaned in close and dropped his voice to a low whisper. "I feel I owe you an explanation on the secret project."

I nodded.

A half-smile tugged at his mouth. "Sorry if I'm being dramatic, but I'll explain tomorrow. There are too many people around here for us to talk. If you'll excuse me, then, I was on my way home." We shook hands, his feeling cold and clammy within my own, before he turned and left. The lanky figure shuffling down the driveway seemed to have aged twenty years since I'd met him a few hours ago.

" 'Three may keep a secret, if two of them are dead,' " a voice whispered to me from the shadows.

Chapter Six

I spun and kicked again. This time the injured toe made contact with a human kneecap.

We both howled.

As I leaned against the garage and waited for the pain-induced nausea to subside, it registered that Max the attorney was walking off his pain by skip-stepping in small circles in the driveway. He looked less scrawny and more brawny dressed in a white T-shirt and baggy workout pants, giving off such a different image than the gray suit of earlier today that I'd been understandably confused.

"What happened?" Sam appeared out of nowhere, her gaze zipping between Max and me.

"Ask her." Max nodded and grimaced in my direction. "I quote some Ben Franklin to her and she whacks me in the knee."

Sam threw me a Queen-Bees-do-not-whack-people look.

"He startled me," I offered in my defense. "But I am sorry, Max." And I was, if only because I'd re-injured my toe. It felt broken now.

"I'm sorry too," he said. His gaze locked with mine, so I assumed he was being sincere.

"Great," Sam said. "Now that that's settled, we need to get down to business. Max, first, thanks for running over on such short notice. We have an emerging situation here, and I didn't think it could wait until tomorrow. We'll make this quick, because we need to get back to our guests. Are you aware that Chief Bennett accused Ellery of Mizizzy's murder?"

"Yes, I am. He doesn't have a shred of evidence. He's just blowing smoke, probably to comfort the residents into thinking he's close to making an arrest."

"So you don't think she did it either?"

"I wasn't sure, until the reading of Ms. Tinsdale's will today." He turned toward me. "Either you're a sorely overlooked candidate for a best-actress Oscar, or your surprise at the inheritance was genuine. I don't see the motive angle."

Another champion in my corner. If I could get these two on the jury, I'd have a sixteen percent chance of being acquitted.

"Is there anything we can do to get Chief Bennett to back down?" Sam asked. Her posture was relaxed, but her thumbs twiddled furiously.

Max stopped exercising his injured leg and stood with his feet shoulder-width apart, his arms extended deep into his pockets. "Since no formal charges have been made, there's no legal course of action to take. But you can be prepared when and if they are."

I liked the idea of having a get-out-of-jail-free card in my pocket, just in case. "How do I do that?" I asked.

"Your attorney can take care of everything," Max said.

"I don't have an attorney."

"Max is the best in town," Sam offered.

"I'm the only one in town, so the competition isn't real stiff."

His modest protests accompanied by a crooked smile got him the job. Along with the fact that maybe he wouldn't sue me for a cracked kneecap if he were my barrister. "You're hired."

"Thank you. I appreciate your business." He dipped his head. "The Eddingtons have overseen the Tinsdales' legal issues for over a hundred years."

"How long have you known that Mizizzy did not die of accidental causes?" Sam asked, forging ahead.

Max shifted uncomfortably under Sam's narrow gaze. "Since the day it happened."

"Why didn't you tell me?"

"I was given a gag order."

"By whom?" Sam and I asked in unison. Great minds think alike.

"Chief Bennett. It's common practice for officials to withhold information if they think it's a significant advantage when interviewing suspects and witnesses."

"As next of kin, is Ellery entitled to any official documents, like the autopsy report or funeral statements?"

"When the police release them, yes. But for what purpose? She doesn't need to prove cause of death in order to inherit, and sometimes those things can be rather graphic. More disturbing than helpful."

"It's for the investigation," Sam said.

Max's eyebrows fused together into one long horizontal stripe. "What investigation?"

"Ellery and I are investigating Mizizzy's murder."

Max laughed. Then he realized it wasn't a joke and coughed over the last few chuckles.

"Attorney-client privilege will prevent you from telling anyone else about this, of course," Sam warned. "It would ruin our cover if anyone knew what we're doing. We need the element of surprise on our side as much as the police."

"Of course." Max shuffled his feet. "No disrespect, Sam, but isn't private investigation a little outside your area of expertise? Now, if I needed someone to organize a backyard barbecue, you would be the first person I'd call. But tracking down killers requires a, ah, different skill set."

Sam's fists settled on her hips, and her foot set to tapping.

"All right. I'll make a few phone calls in the morning. Miss Tinsdale, I'll give you an update when you arrive for your appointment."

"Great. Thanks, Max. We owe you one." Sam spoke for both of us.

"Promise me one thing, though. You'll be very careful and go straight to the police with any information you find. This person has already shown his disregard for human life."

Hmm. Dire warning taken seriously. At least by me. I nodded fervently.

Sam made no such promise.

After a quick washup at the kitchen sink, I rejoined Sam at our table. I was delighted to find a slice of caramel-and-chocolate-chip cheesecake waiting for me. Even though I was full to bursting, anything chocolatey, caramely, and cheesy is good for what ails you. And my toe still ailed me something fierce.

"Sit. Eat," Sam ordered. "The men went to smoke stogies. We can go over everything we've found out so far."

Before I'd so much as settled myself into my dessert-eating position, a woman joined us. My fork poised mid-first-bite as I stared as what could best be described as Uncle Sam's wife. She was dressed from head to toe in red, white, and blue, and had gone crazy with the BeDazzler. Fake rhinestones studded the low V-neck T-shirt, drawing attention to her pruny cleavage. Her hair could be illustrated in beauty school training manuals on how there is such a thing as too much henna. But it was her earrings that gave me pause—silver stars the size of CDs. My own lobes hurt just looking at them.

The woman sat down and attacked her double serving of cheesecake with gusto, and I decided I liked her.

Sam introduced our new tablemate as Doris Rogers, wife of Doodles (the "round" man) and, hence, my across-the-street neighbor.

Once the formalities were over, I tucked into my own slice of chocolate/caramel heaven.

"You'll love Lorraine's cheesecake," Doris said between bites. "It's won first prize at the county fair seven years running." Doris closed her eyes and quivered with so much gastronomic pleasure her cleavage undulated and threatened to ooze out over the rhinestones.

"Lorraine is Connie's wife," Sam informed me. "She's the woman standing by the dessert table over there talking to Mayor Twiddy."

I glanced over my shoulder and choked on a chocolate chip when I identified Connie's wife as the tall, thin woman with waist-length blond hair. She was dressed more appropriately for a downtown Cleveland street corner than a Braddocks Beach potluck. She wore a sheer blouse that allowed a clear view of a lacey bra, and a red-denim miniskirt that served the same purpose as a neon sign, sending out a message impossible to ignore. Also impossible to ignore were the long, coltish legs that stretched down into scarlet canvas sandals. I didn't need to see the toenails to know they were painted to match her shoes. She ran her tongue over her puffy red lips in a none-too-subtle invitation to be kissed, but Mayor Twiddy just laughed at her.

"Do either of you know anything about guns?" Sam asked in a droll tone of voice usually reserved for nice-day-isn't-it small talk. "I'm trying to figure out if Mizizzy was killed by a shotgun or a handgun."

My attention flitted from Lorraine to Doris, who stopped chewing with her chin in the downward position. She stared at Sam and made a production out of swallowing before asking, "Miss Izzy was shot? With a gun?"

"Yes."

"How awful. A shooting. Less than a hundred yards from where I sleep."

I'd read about them, but I'd never actually witnessed a woman suffer a case of the vapors. The back-of-the-hand-to-the-forehead and the bobblehead motion had me making a mental bet whether she'd land facedown in the cheesecake or toes-to-heaven on the lawn. Sam reached across the table and waved the plate of cheesecake under Doris' nose as if it were smelling salts. That seemed to do the trick.

"It must have had a silencer, or we would have heard it," Sam continued, as if we hadn't just almost lost Doris. "Can shotguns have silencers? I wonder if we can get our hands on the pictures to analyze the blood-splatter patterns."

So much for polite after-dinner conversation. I pushed my unfinished dessert away.

"Where were *you* at two o'clock on the morning of May thirtieth?" Sam's steely gaze settled on Doris. "You didn't happen to hear anything unusual that night, did you?"

Doris didn't answer.

"Talk to me, Doris. This is important. The police need to find Mizizzy's killer. Now, tell me if you saw anything unusual that night." Sam had her elbows on the table, hands folded as if in prayer, tapping her thumbs against her lips while waiting for Doris' response. And wait we did.

Eventually, Doris' chest no longer heaved with every breath, and her color returned to its normal splotchiness. I couldn't tell by her facial expression if she were giving Sam's question serious consideration or thinking about the best way to carry home the uneaten half of the cheesecake. After what seemed like an hour, Doris spoke. "Let me think. May thirtieth was the day of the uptown beautification project. We'd hauled and spread two thousand cubic yards of mulch. Every muscle in my body ached. Must have been about eight o'clock I took three Motrin and went to bed."

"When did you first realize something was wrong?"

"When the red lights started flashing in our bedroom."

"Did you go out to see what was going on?" Sam pressured the witness.

"You know I did, Samantha," Doris snapped. "You were already standing out there when I got there."

"Did you get close enough to see the body?" The tone of Sam's voice had me wondering if she'd done a stint as a drill sergeant.

Doris sat up straighter and answered the question. "You know I didn't. Nobody did. The police kept us all away."

"Did you hear any gunshots?"

"No. Nothing." Doris pushed what was left of her cheese-cake away.

"Any idea why Mizizzy would have visited the watchtower in the middle of the night?"

"I do know she'd been having trouble sleeping lately. Had something on her mind, she'd said. Sometimes she took a walk. Sometimes she watched infomercials."

"Did she tell you what was on her mind?"

"No, she didn't. Said she didn't want to talk about it. You know me, Sam. I don't like to pry."

Sam snorted.

Doris sniffed. "I don't. Can I help it that I'm a good listener and people open up to me all the time? It's a curse, I tell you."

I let my mind wander. Sam had raised a good question. Had Aunt Izzy gone to the watchtower of her own free will? And if so, why? Not to see the clouds, not at that time of night. Sam said it was often used as a lovers' trysting place. Maybe Aunt Izzy had been meeting someone? Or maybe she'd stumbled onto someone else's secret rendezvous? One that wasn't necessarily concerned with affairs of the heart? Maybe a drug deal gone awry or something else that made someone think she was better off dead than alive?

Sam's raised voice brought my attention back to the conversation. "Come on, Doris. You're hiding something. Spill it."

"Well, Doodles—"

"What? Doodles what? Tell me!"

"Doodles said—"

"Doodles said what?"

"Doodles said he heard something earlier that night."

"What did he hear?"

"Voices. People talking."

"Did he hear what they said?"

"Yes."

"What did Doodles hear, Doris?"

I thought for a moment that Sam was going to crawl across the table, wrap Doris in a headlock, and threaten her with a noogie until she talked.

"Doodles said he heard someone talking when he went to close the windows that night."

"What time was that?"

"He usually comes to bed right after Jay Leno's monologue, so about eleven forty-five."

"What? What did he hear?"

"He heard someone say, 'One of us is going to have to kill him.'"

Sam and I gasped in unison.

"Him? Not her?" Sam whispered.

"Doodles definitely said 'him.'"

"Are you sure?"

Doris nodded her head.

"But that doesn't make sense. Why *him* and not *her?*" Sam seemed to be thinking aloud, and Doris and I let her babble. "Were they talking about someone other than Mizizzy? Did they kill the wrong person? Was she just in the wrong place at the wrong time? Is another person on the list who will be killed? A *him?*" Sam tapped her fingers on the table while staring into the sky. Her gaze dropped and locked on Doris. "Did Doodles see who was talking?"

"He said he looked out the window, but he couldn't see anyone."

"Did he recognize the voice?"

Doris turned and looked over her shoulder.

"Doris."

Doris looked back at Sam, but didn't say anything.

"Doris," Sam growled through clenched teeth. "If you don't tell me who Doodles heard talking, I swear I'm going to tell everyone in this town that you use Prego in your, quote, 'made-from-my-Granny-Rosario's, may she rest in peace,' secret recipe."

I can't say that I approved of Sam's interrogation techniques, but they seemed to work.

Doris glanced around and then leaned in toward the center of the table. Sam and I leaned in too.

"It was Lorraine Littleton."

Chapter Seven

The screams that followed Doris' statement did not come from me. Nor from Sam. The scream that turned my blood to ice came from Lorraine herself, from where she stood between the dessert table and one of the picked-over dining tables.

Our heads swiveled in unison to see the cause of the commotion. Standing inches from Lorraine was a tall woman with long black hair parted down the middle, Morticia Addams–style. She had cheesecake dripping from her face and a look that indicated she was one impulse away from ripping Lorraine's eyeballs from their sockets.

Sam brushed past me and raced toward the melee. Not one to miss a good catfight, I hustled along behind to make sure I had a front-row seat.

Sam stopped short of the two women. I didn't. The law of gross tonnage never fails, and I bumped poor Sam right into the middle of things just as Lorraine let loose with a cup of strawberry margarita. I grimaced at the pink liquid bleeding into Sam's white polka dots. The crowd murmured its sympathy as Sam dabbed ineffectively at the stains.

Lorraine became the focus of everyone's attention again when she let loose a maniacal laugh. "You wicked little witch!" She elbowed Sam out of her way. "How dare you?" This time, a plate of discarded chicken bones and uneaten potato salad flew into the face of the accusee. "Mayor Twiddy just told me he saw you sneaking out the back door of my house! My house! You have no business in my house!"

"It's Connie's house just as much as it is yours." The woman flicked her head, spraying bits of food onto those within a two-foot perimeter.

Lorraine gasped. "You were in there *with* Connie? Why? What business do you have with *my* husband? I want answers, Betty Anne. And I want them now!" She clenched her fist and took a menacing step toward the woman.

"Lorraine," Sam said in a calming voice as she put a restraining hand against Lorraine's shoulder. "I'm sure Betty Anne had a very reasonable explanation for being in your house. Don't you, Betty Anne?"

"Yes, I do."

The music stopped. The whispers stopped. The sound of leaves rustling in the breeze stopped. Silence held while the crowd waited for Betty Anne to elaborate.

"Well?" Sam prompted.

Lorraine raised her fist in front of her own nose, her middle knuckle protruding forward from the rest, like street fighters do in order to inflict more pain and injury when all the force focuses on the one point of impact instead of being spread across four digits. "I swear if you boinked Connie—" Lorraine bounced around, punching the air in a way that reminded me of the cowardly lion in the *Wizard of Oz*. False bravado.

I took one step backward and glanced around the crowd. Most of the spectators seemed appalled. Some seemed nervous. One seemed amused—Mayor Twiddy. In fact, he seemed more than amused; he was downright gleeful.

"That's a question for Connie to answer. All I can say is it's not what you think," Betty Anne said.

"What I think is that you're having an affair with my husband." Lorraine lunged for Betty Anne. Sam lunged for Lorraine. Doris lunged for Sam and tugged her back into the safety of the crowd.

A red-bearded man stepped forward and pulled the two women apart. He tucked Betty Anne behind him and stepped toward Lorraine, spewing threats of opening cans of whoop-ass and insults against people's mothers.

Lorraine gave as good as she got, both verbally and with

food. She tossed everything she could get her hands on, but she was a terrible shot, even at point-blank range. Betty Anne emerged from her bunker to return volley with a shotgun spray of baked-bean bullets, then slipped back behind her protector.

Shouts broke out, as people seemed to take sides. More people threw food. Gourmet pasta salad flew through the air. Burger buns. Brownies. Shrimp cocktail. Broccoli slaw landed on my new sandals and its vinegar juice oozed through my toes.

Things were just on the brink of total collapse when somebody fired a gun.

Instinct had me diving for cover under the nearest table, although I can't explain why I thought the plastic resin would offer me much protection against a metal slug. I held my breath, waiting for more screams or gunshots, but all I heard was silence. An odd, eerie silence that left my skin feeling clammy. I peeked from under the table and found the hostess and her guests all staring at Chief Bennett, who stood on top of a table in the middle of the crowd, blowing smoke from the barrel of his gun. He smiled at the townsfolk.

Sam was the first to speak. "Is that what they teach you in the big city? Shoot first and ask questions later?"

Chief Bennett looked at Mayor Twiddy. Mayor Twiddy looked at the crowd. The crowd waited for something; I'm not sure what. I crawled out to better observe the drama unfolding like a Wild West stunt show.

Sam spoke again. "You had better thank your lucky stars that you didn't injure or, worse, kill anyone with that stupid trick."

"These folks were rioting."

"These folks were having a civilized food fight. Big difference. One whoop of your siren would have quieted everyone back down."

As Sam and the chief argued over preferred methods of crowd control, a movement on the fringes of the pack drew my attention. It was Lorraine, tiptoeing toward the gate. My Nancy Drew impulse kicked in and I tiptoed after her, but by the time I reached the street, she was speeding past me in a sleek, low-slung, Mars-red Mercedes SLK350 convertible, her long blond hair whipping in the wind. With my hands on my hips, I stood watching as the taillights disappeared north up Charleston Avenue.

I returned to Sam's backyard and found Mayor Twiddy and George Greene holding a tête-à-tête in the shadows of the garage. Betty Anne sat in a chair near the deck, picking macaroni salad from her hair. Sam stood behind with her hands on the distraught woman's shoulders. The red-bearded man knelt at Betty Anne's feet, trying to coerce her to take a drink from a plastic margarita cup.

Activity buzzed around the rest of the yard as men stacked tables and chairs in the back of a pickup truck and women circled round the food table, burping Tupperware or crimping foil over casserole dishes.

One key player was noticeably absent in the well-choreographed Cleanup Ballet, and that was the man with the gun, Chief Bennett. I just hoped he wasn't out in search of evidence to arrest me for Aunt Izzy's murder.

Chapter Eight

It turns out there *was* a test on the names of the partygoers that evening. I failed. Miserably.

As Sam walked me to the gate in front of Aunt Izzy's house, she asked, "Don't you think Scootch McKenzie hesitated just a little bit when we asked her where she was during the late hours of May thirtieth?" We stopped in the circle of light cast by a reproduction gas lamp. She pulled her classic black cardigan with tiny pearly buttons so that the two ends overlapped. With her arms crossed to hold it in place, she effectively hid the strawberry margarita stains from my view.

"What kind of name is Scootch?"

"Her real name is . . . Geez, I don't think I even know. She's been known as Scootch since she was a baby. Never learned to crawl, just sat on her bottom and scootched her way across the floor."

"How old is she?"

"Two years away from retirement is all I know. Maybe sixty-eight?"

"Do people ever outgrow their childhood nicknames here?"

"Never."

I'd best be careful not to be tagged with some crazy name I'd never live to outgrow. "Which one was Scootch?"

"The one wearing the Brunello Cucinelli cashmere cardigan."

I racked my brain to recall a Brunello Cucinelli sweater. Who was I fooling? I wouldn't know one if Brunello himself wrapped it around my shoulders.

"The Lilly Pulitzer wrap skirt?"

I gave her an I-don't-know-what-you're-talking-about shoulder shrug and smile.

"The cute Dolce and Gabbana slides?"

I shook my head and sighed. Couture-speak was lost on me.

Sam sighed in return. Loudly. "The fair-skinned woman with the big mole on her neck."

Now her, I remembered. She ought to have that thing removed. "What about her?"

"Did you think she might be hiding something?"

"Hard to tell. She seemed distracted. Wasn't someone else talking to her at the same time? Something about the church rummage sale next weekend?"

"Oh, you're right. She's the Ways and Means chairperson for the Church of Divine Spiritual Enlightenment. Mizizzy was a member there. How much did she bequeath to them?"

"Half a million, I think."

"Their new building is supposed to cost a lot more than that. A couple of mil, if memory serves. Scootch is going to have to do a whole lot of rummaging." Sam's voice trailed off and the sound of her foot tapping against the sidewalk filled the night air. "What about Veralee Leinhart?"

"Who's she?"

"She was wearing—" Sam stopped herself and seemed to choose her words very carefully. "The one whose bangs flop to the tip of her nose, and she's always blowing them out of the way when she talks."

Ah, yes. I'd dubbed her The Sheepdog. "What about her?"

"Her husband was out of town tonight, so you didn't get to meet him, but he plays poker with the town coroner. I asked her if she'd seen or heard anything unusual, but it didn't even occur to me to ask her if she knew anything about the autopsy report. Nuts." Sam pounded the side of her head with the heel of her hand. "I have a lot to learn about investigating. We'll have to schedule a visit to her gift shop tomorrow. It's going to be a very busy day. Don't forget our seven A.M. breakfast meeting with Mystic Sayers from the Tri-B."

Oops, I had forgotten. Wait. No, I hadn't forgotten. This was the first I'd heard of it.

"Tinky's serves a three-egg omelet with tomatoes and peppers and some secret seasoning that's out of this world. I'll knock on your door about six forty-five. Do you have something to wear? She'll probably want photos."

I thought about my clean or dirty T-shirt options and shook my head.

"Make that six fifteen, then, and I'll scrounge up something. With all the social obligations these next few days, we may have to squeeze a shopping trip in sometime tomorrow, but I don't see how."

I learned long ago my double-X chromosomes don't carry the shopping gene. There was nothing I hated more than a trip to the mall. And add Sam and her Tasmanian devilish energy force to that, and it promised to be an excruciatingly painful event. I'd have to think of an excuse to beg off.

We said our good nights, and I thanked Sam for the party and for all she'd done for me today. She waved my comments off, then reached in and hugged me. I wrapped my arms around her slight body and went through the motions. That was another gene I lacked, the compassionate-friend one.

"I felt so certain we'd find something out tonight. But don't despair. We're going to find Mizizzy's killer," Sam whispered. "As long as there is breath in our bodies, we'll keep searching." With a sniffle, she turned, tucked her head down, and scurried down the sidewalk to her house.

I didn't like the sound of that "breath in our bodies" comment, in light of the fact that we were, as Max had so eloquently put it, dealing with someone who had already proved he had no regard for human life. Before I could clarify my commitment, Sam had buzzed off home.

After staring down the quiet street for a few moments, I turned and starting walking. My fingers trailed along the white pickets of Aunt Izzy's front-yard fence. *Ka-thump, ka-thump, ka-thump.* I strolled past the gate and along to the corner.

Gazing across Braddocks Boulevard at the lake shimmering in the moonlight, I contemplated the changes my life had undergone in the past few hours. Still wrapped in the camaraderic cocoon of the potluck, I had a feeling of belonging here. But what weighed heavily on my mind was the inheritance. Amounts of money in the eight digits would change not only my life, but me. Living in this town for five years and learning about my heritage would redefine me. Being a multimillionaire would elevate me to a new social class, separating me from the hardworking, middle-class people I'm comfortable with. And spending money earned by the blood, sweat, and tears of ancestors I'd never met, never even knew existed, went against every self-respecting bone in my body. But who in their right mind would give up something like this? After all, there was plenty of money to go around, and I could do a lot of good things with it.

The cool night air and an overwhelming sense of responsibility whispered down my arms, and I shivered.

Turning, I studied the lonely house that could one day be mine, nestled under a canopy of statuesque maple trees. While waiting for my clothes to arrive from Chiquita, I'd wandered through the rooms, touched some heirlooms, and glanced through the titles on the bookshelf, but I hadn't felt a connection with Aunt Izzy. I felt a need to understand this woman, both her life and her death.

Some invisible thread drew me diagonally across the street toward the watchtower where Aunt Izzy had been murdered. The full-moon light played peekaboo behind clouds, giving me glimpses of a conical, sandstone structure situated halfway between the street and the water's edge. The wind picked up, pushing Lake Braddock against the shore in white-capped ankle-beaters. Sailboats groaned against their piers. Lanyards clanged against metal masts in a maritime symphony that I usually found soothing. But not tonight. Unsettling would be more accurate.

I slipped my sandals off, hooked my thumb through the

heel straps, and walked barefoot across the beach. With the sun having set a few hours earlier, the sand was cool, almost cold, and so deep that walking was difficult.

The sandstone tower absorbed the moonlight, giving it an ethereal appearance. I circled the three-story-tall, eight-sided, windowless structure, studying it from all angles while trying to define the sensations rolling through my body. Heart-pounding, hands-shaking, knees-knocking sensations caused by more than a solitary stroll along an unfamiliar beach at the witching hour. I knew something evil lurked in the building's hollow darkness as sure as I knew the sun would rise the next morning.

My head wanted to turn and run, but my feet failed me as they scratched of their own accord along the wooden ramp leading from the beach to the watchtower's entrance. I approached the door with trepidation, reminding myself I was being silly to think I might find Aunt Izzy's dead body on the other side. The crime scene had been cleared and her body properly buried more than a week ago.

Despite my protests, my hand reached out and grasped the cold brass doorknob. With a twist and a tug, the large wooden door creaked outward. My feet carried me across the threshold and into the cavernous, darker-than-sin chamber. The door slammed shut behind me, and I jumped against the lonely sound echoing off the chamber's walls. I paused, waiting for my eyes to adjust to the small amount of moonlight that beckoned to me from the opening to the crow's nest far above. My gaze followed the iron staircase, spiraling down around the perimeter of the tower to where it ended just inches from my toes. I edged forward cautiously, and stopped at the foot of the stairs to take a deep breath. The air smelled musty, like a damp basement. But there was more to it. A coppery smell that could only be blood. Human blood. So strong I could taste it on my lips.

It was a tug-o-wills, as I tried my darndest not to go. But the invisible thread had more weight on its side, which meant it must be some formidable force. Slowly, one narrow step at a time, I circled my way to the top of the watchtower.

My heart hammered in an increasingly frenetic triplet/rest pattern as I neared the pinnacle. My mind added the lyrics to the beat: *Ell-er-y, pause. Ell-er-y, pause. Ell-er-y, pause.*

As I stepped onto the landing that led to the outer viewing area, the message changed. *Go-home-now, pause. Go-home-now, pause. Go-home-now, pause.* I hadn't lived to see my forty-eighth year on this earth by ignoring my inner voice.

I turned and hightailed it out of there. One hand gripping the iron handrail and the other pressed against the rough sandstone wall, I raced down the steps two at a time. I misjudged the bottom and tripped down the last four risers but, more through luck than athletic agility, managed to keep myself upright.

It was more than my heartbeat talking to me now. A voice, not quite human, echoed endlessly within the walls of the tower. It rose to a primeval shriek, louder and more otherworldly with every second. It seemed to reach inside of me in an attempt to wrench my soul from my body.

I panicked.

My hands fumbled with the doorknob, but it was as if somebody had covered it with Crisco. I grabbed harder and managed to turn it. I reared back and pulled with all my might. But it wouldn't budge. I was trapped inside with some sort of poltergeist who was trying to pull me over to the dark side.

A cold breeze whispered across the back of my neck and down my spine. I tried to dodge it and in the process stumbled forward. With a woeful protest, the door swung out into the night. It barely registered in my scared-stupid brain that I'd been trying to pull the door inward when it opened outward.

I ran down the ramp, hit the deep sand at Mach 1 speed, and raced across the beach with my arms windmilling for all I was worth. The scream still followed me, still taunted me, still terrorized me. Halfway to the road I realized the shriek was coming from my own throat, but I couldn't seem to stop.

My plan was to run all the way home—to Virginia Beach.

Something stopped me, and it wasn't until I heard the grunt from beneath my sprawled body that I realized I'd trampled a person. Not just any person. Chief Bennett. Again.

"Are you hell-bent on flattening me into a pancake or something?"

I rolled to the side and sank into the sand. The collision seemed to have knocked the screams from me, and now all I could hear was my heavy breathing, the chief's heavy breathing, and the sound of the waves in the distance.

The chief sat up and brushed sand from his hair and shoulders.

"I . . . I . . . I . . ." The words just wouldn't come out.

"What the hell's wrong with you, woman? You're acting as if you'd seen a ghost or something."

"I . . . I . . . I . . ."

"Just what are you up to, anyway?"

I closed my gaping mouth and gathered my thoughts. "I . . . I . . . I just wanted to see the watchtower."

"Returning to the scene of the crime, huh?"

"Y-y-yes. Yes."

"Aha. I knew it. You just admitted it. You killed Isabel."

"No. No." *I was visiting the scene of the crime for the first time. Something drew me here. Something I couldn't explain,* I wanted to yell. The words collected on the tip of my tongue but couldn't get past my lips.

"I'm booking you on murder." Chief Bennett struggled against the sand until he got his feet underneath him. "You have the right to remain silent," he said as he pulled my arms behind my back and slapped handcuffs on my wrists. "Anything you say can and will be used against you in a court of law."

Not a problem. My brain-to-mouth connection seemed to have been severed.

"You have the right to an attorney—"

I sure hoped Max made middle-of-the-night jail calls.

"If you cannot afford one, one will be appointed for you. Do you understand?"

The only thing I understood was that walking barefoot in the sand with hands cuffed behind your back, on legs that had expended all their energy running from a close encounter of the ghostly kind, was only possible if somebody held you roughly by the upper arm to keep you from falling on your face. I wasn't sure who was breathing harder, Chief Bennett or me, when we finally reached his police cruiser.

Through the miracle of small-town communication systems, Max beat me to the station, limiting my time in the lockup to three minutes and seventeen seconds. Chief Bennett was forced to release me upon Max's presentation of sworn affidavits. The first was from a co-worker, the second a neighbor, and the third a waitress at my favorite restaurant. All swore to having seen me between seven P.M. and midnight on May 30 in Virginia Beach, providing me alibis for the time of Aunt Izzy's death.

I didn't want to appear ungrateful by telling them I'd never heard of any of those women.

Chapter Nine

Anything less than eight hours of uninterrupted sleep and I'm a bear to deal with. When my alarm clock sounded at six A.M., exactly two hours and forty-three minutes since the last time I'd looked at it, I knew it was going to be a bad day for all concerned.

It didn't help that Sam was Miss Merry Sunshine when she came tiptoeing into my bedroom. "Get up, get up. The dew's on the buttercup."

"No." I pulled the covers over my head and mentally wrote a yellow sticky note to myself to have all the locks on the house changed.

I should have realized Sam wasn't the type to take no for an answer.

"Chiquita found a rose-colored silk blouse that will bring out the color in your cheeks. I hope the black pants aren't too short."

I snuggled down deeper under the covers.

Sam yanked the comforter down.

I clenched my eyes against the sunshine, daggers of pain shooting to the back of my head. Sam must have opened the blinds, because I'd twisted them as tight as they would go last night in order to avoid just such a scenario. I cracked open one eye and looked around. A whisper of a breeze blew the daisy-print café curtains into the room. When I'd staked my claim yesterday, the yellow, black, and white theme had seemed cheerful. This morning, it made me want to strangle someone. And that someone was Sam. Not just because she'd opened the blinds, but because she looked so party-perfect in her tropical-fish-print sarong and white sandals, with her hair pulled into a sassy ponytail. Nobody should look so put together at this ungodly hour.

I buried my head deep under the covers and mumbled, "Go away, Sam."

"Your Aunt Izzy always said, ' 'Tis better to greet the day with Good morning, Lord, not Good lord, morning.'" The covers came off again, and I felt myself being rolled to a semi-sitting position. My bare feet hit the cool hardwood floor. Next thing I knew, I was standing.

"I'll hang your clothes in the bathroom, and you can get a quick shower. Then we can talk while I fix your hair. I did a lot of thinking last night."

So had I. Too much, which is why it had taken me more than three hours to get to sleep after my midnight visit to the jail.

With about as much enthusiasm as a woman heading for a root canal, I shuffled toward the door.

"Where are your shoes?"

"Down at the watchtower." At least, that's the last time I remembered having had them in my hand.

Sam gave me a puzzled look. I stifled her with a don't-even-ask glare.

She left me to my business, calling over her shoulder, "I'll be back in ten minutes."

Thanks for the warning.

I sleepwalked my way through my morning ministrations, buttoned my blouse wrong, twice, and almost brushed my teeth with athlete's foot cream. I needed coffee. Preferably delivered via a direct IV hookup.

Sam joined me in the powder-puff pink and battleship gray bathroom. "You look great. And look what I found."

I looked. My shoes dangled from her hand, a bit sandy but no worse for their night on the beach. "Thanks." At least that's what I'd intended to say. It sounded more like "Hrumphhh" to my own ears. I returned to my task of slipping silver hoop earrings into my lobes. Not easy to do, when my fingers didn't respond to what messages my brain sent their way. I needed sleep and caffeine, not necessarily in that order.

"Chiquita's such a jewel. Since we don't have time to go shopping, she's going to have some more outfits delivered so you can try them on at your leisure. I told them to send the bill to Max's office, since I assume you'll leave him in charge of your assets, the way Mizizzy had."

Dollar signs marqueed their way across my brain. It might take all my Alaskan cruise money to settle that score. I sighed, not having the mental energy to think about financial matters at the moment.

"Sit here." Sam motioned to a small chrome stool. A very small chrome stool with a pillbox cushion. I perched atop it, summoning instant sympathy for circus elephants that are made to sit on ten-sizes-too-small, star-painted platforms. "I'll do your hair," she said. "A little gel to lift it off your face a bit. I'll make an appointment with Renaldo to have it colored."

"No."

"No color?"

"Nope. I am who I am, and I intend to stay that way."

"I admire that." Her tone belied the words.

Sam rubbed some gel between her hands, and the room filled with the aroma of raspberries on steroids. Using her fingers, she forked it through my hair while talking at her usual mile-a-minute pace. "Lorraine has a drinking problem and tipped back one too many margaritas last night."

Gee, tell me something I didn't know.

"She doesn't usually get violent, though. The accusations of Connie and Betty Anne shocked us all. Lorraine and Connie are the poster children for wedded bliss here in Braddocks Beach. But *in vino veritas,* and all that. Maybe things aren't all the good between them. There was a bad patch when Lorraine's drinking problem was at its peak, but she's been dry for over ten years. I wonder why she fell off the wagon last night? Maybe she'd been pushed." Sam plugged the hair dryer in and began styling my short tresses.

I thought about the conundrum that was the Littletons'

marriage. "What did Connie ever see in Lorraine?" I yelled to be heard above the whistling air, but it came out harsher than I'd planned.

"What do you mean?"

Hmm. How to phrase this without offending anyone. "Connie seems so cultured, and Lorraine, well, *cheap* is the word that comes to mind."

Sam laughed. "Lorraine's just going through a phase right now. A midlife crisis of sorts. She tossed her pearls and Anne Klein suits out with the leftover deviled eggs last Easter and has been reinventing herself as a *young thaannng* ever since. I agree that last night's outfit was a bit over the top, and I suspect Connie talked to her about it. After all, her image reflects on him also. I did hear through the grapevine that she's seeing a therapist up in Cleveland. I suspect this will all be over by the time the snow flies."

While Sam dried my hair, I thought about snow. I had an allergy to it. Not that I went into apoplectic shock or anything, but I developed an itchy rash that lasted until the temperature returned to the sixty-degree range. Five winters in Braddocks Beach . . . I scratched the prickly feeling spreading from the base of my neck.

"Did I tell you Lorraine and Betty Anne are in-laws-to-be? Lorraine and Connie's daughter Cordelia, or Cordy for short, is engaged to Betty Anne's oldest son. I'm sure you'll be invited to the wedding, you being local royalty and all. There's nothing this town does better than a good wedding. Except a good funeral, of course, and Mizizzy's was the best of the best . . ." Sam's voice trailed off.

She dug the brush into my scalp and tugged my hair so hard my head yanked to the left. "Ouch! Careful there. That's attached to me."

"Sorry, El."

"Ellery," I corrected her. The longer I was awake, the shorter my temper became.

Sam finished styling my hair in silence, which was okay by me.

We headed out into the crisp morning air and walked the few short blocks to town, Sam pointing out landmarks as we went.

"Have you had much time to read up on Braddocks Beach history?"

"Not since last night, no," I said.

"Our founding fathers were big Revolutionary War buffs, and when they laid out the streets, they named them in order of the battles. Lexington through Yorktown, with Tinsdale Circle being the exception."

We reached the town hub and turned southwest along the road named after my ancestor. Our destination, Tinky's, was diametrically across the town circle from Reba's Pie-ery. Sam held the door open, and I entered the dimly lit restaurant.

As modernly nostalgic as Reba's had been, Tinky's was authentically so. The floor was utilitarian linoleum, its original color anyone's guess. The walls were about three shades lighter on the unidentifiable color chart. Old wooden chairs, grimy with years of airborne cooking grease, were arranged around tables with noticeable tilts. Ceramic-cow cream dispensers and dried-out baskets filled with sugar and sweetener packets vied for space with red and yellow squeeze-bottle condiment dispensers at the center of the tables.

The aroma of coffee raised my spirits. A steaming cup appeared under my nose before my backside even hit the chair, bless the waitress' heart. Two sugars and a splash of cream later, I had caffeine surging through my body and began to feel human again.

"After Mystic's done interviewing you, we'll do a little interviewing of our own. This woman knows everything, and I mean everything, that goes on in this town." Sam's eyes lifted for just a second, and she smiled. One of those plastered-on fake smiles often seen on the paparazzi pictures in fanzines.

Sam rose and whispered out of the corner of her mouth, "Just follow my lead." With enough phony enthusiasm to garner an Emmy nod, she gushed, "Mystic. We're so glad you could join us this morning."

A woman dressed in tattered jeans and a T-shirt that proclaimed ALL STRESSED OUT AND NO ONE TO CHOKE brushed past Sam and honed in on me. Her dozen or so silver bracelets jingled softly as we shook hands. "You must be El."

"She prefers to be called Ellery," Sam said.

"Ellery it is. I'm Mystic." The woman suffered the lifelong effects of too much daytime sun and nighttime whiskey. After the past ten years in a beach-party environment, I was somewhat of an expert on the subject myself, so I deducted ten years from her appearance and judged her to be in her late thirties.

We settled in our seats and ordered. I took Sam's suggestion for the Tinky's Special, the omelet with secret seasonings. I added two slices of buttered white toast and settled for home fries after the waitress had narrowed her eyes in bewilderment when I'd asked for grits.

Before the waitress had written everything down, Mystic started up with some hard-hitting questions about the food fight at Sam's house last night. Sam remained tight-lipped. I followed her lead, as instructed.

"Well, so much for a front-page scoop," Mystic said as she delved her hand into the depths of her backpack. "Guess that leaves us with the story of Braddocks Beach's newest resident. Mind if I tape this?" Without waiting for consent, she pulled a small recorder from her backpack and set it on the table. "So tell me about your life in Virginia Beach." Boredom dripped from her voice.

Before I could begin my life story, the waitress delivered plates piled high with breakfast offerings. The steam spiraling off the eggs was fragrant and kicked my saliva glands into high gear.

A cell phone rang in the vicinity, chiming an electronic version of Jimmy Buffet's "Margaritaville." Mystic jumped in her seat, reached for her bag, and began digging. Before the melody got to the *lost shaker of salt* part, she had it snapped open and up to her ear. "Sayers. Speak."

Mystic's face paled as she grabbed the tape recorder and

shoved it into the backpack. "Got it," she said into the phone, then to us, "Sorry to run. There's breaking news over on Charleston Avenue."

"What's up?" Sam asked as she took her first bite of pancakes.

"They just found Connie Littleton lying in a pool of blood."

Chapter Ten

Sam's fork clattered to the table as she jumped from her chair and raced out of Tinky's in Mystic's wake. "Put that on Miss Tinsdale's tab," she called to the confused waitress. "And give yourself a big tip."

I looked longingly at my untouched breakfast and half-full cup of coffee, but my concern for Connie outweighed my need for sustenance. Throwing my napkin on the counter, I gave chase to Sam and Mystic. I caught up with them on the sidewalk where Tindsale Circle intersected with Ticonderoga. Sam held open both doors of a black, snarling-expressioned Excursion and motioned me to hurry up. I scrambled in the back as quickly as I could. Sam slammed my door.

Before Sam could get all the way into the car herself, Mystic punched the accelerator and the Excursion lunged forward.

We sped through the streets, with the passenger door still open and Sam standing on the running board. If we made a left turn, centrifugal force would throw her off. I held my breath. Fortunately, the drive consisted of two right turns, both taken at an alarming speed.

Sam must have one fast-flying guardian angel, because we made it to Charleston Street without mishap.

The house with the four police cars and one ambulance parked along the circular driveway must be the Littletons'. It was a beautiful home, a two-story Georgian, whose painted-white bricks were barely discernible through the thick covering of ivy. It was the type of home from which fairy tales spring. But based on the grim expressions of the civil servants milling about, this story was not going to have a happy ending.

The truck bumped over the curb and stopped with its grille kissing the white picket fence. Mystic slammed it into park. She and Sam were off and running before the truck stopped rocking.

After I managed to get the child-locked door opened, I was off and running too, with no particular destination. I skittered to a stop at the edge of the white picket fence and took in the scene. A significant crowd had gathered along the street, and it probably outnumbered the civil servants by about three to one. Mystic stood in the middle of the yard under a spreading chestnut tree. Her cell phone was tucked between her shoulder and ear as she scribbled notes on her notepad while talking to two police officers. Sam was over by the garage, rocking a distraught young woman in her arms. It didn't take Sherlock Holmes to deduce that the woman who looked like a young, chunkier, but more demurely dressed version of Lorraine was Connie and Lorraine's daughter. An unusual name. Dordy? Corky? Cordy! That was it. She looked devastated. No, that was an understatement. The poor young woman looked as if someone had taken all forty-six miles of nerves out of her body, run them through a meat grinder, and then stuffed them back in so that nothing connected in the way it was supposed to and the whole system was short circuiting on every level.

A slight movement drew my eye to a camera lens the length of my arm poking over the fence near the garage. It was pointed in Cordy's direction, documenting the most heart-wrenching and private of moments. Suspecting they'd be selling the pictures for profit, a burning anger surged through my body. The poor girl had the right to grieve in peace. And since nobody else seemed interested in stopping it, it was up to me.

I took off at a trot and soon was pounding the ground toward the intrusive camera lens. I am not light on my feet, not by any stretch of the imagination, and I waved my arms and screamed like the girl that I was, in hopes of distracting the cameraman.

When I was within twenty-five feet, the camera turned in my direction. An unctuous smile spread across the photographer's face as he snapped my picture. That angered me even more. My only thought as I prepared to pounce on the Weeble-shaped man was that *Queen Bees don't attack small-town paparazzi.*

The photographer turned to run but tripped and fell smack on his round belly. I took advantage of his diminished capacity to wrest the camera from his hands. In this age of digital cameras, I did not have the drama of opening up the back and exposing the roll of film to the light, nor did I have the time to figure out how to delete the pictures. For lack of a third option, I heaved the heavy camera as if I'd been competing for an Olympic gold metal in the shot put.

It landed with a satisfying thunk in the road, just as a fire engine roared to the scene. The photographer yelled as his apparatus was reduced to small silver and black smithereens.

He threatened me with every lawsuit in the book, and I told him to contact my lawyer and beat a hasty retreat. I hoped Max had some expertise in this area, because the froth foaming around the edges of the photographer's mouth led me to believe he would make good on every one of his threats. I felt confident that my desire to protect Cordy's privacy would tip the scales of justice in my favor. No worries.

Yes, worries. I spotted Sam stomping across the lawn, looking ready to kill someone. And that someone seemed to be me.

I turned to run, but she grabbed me by the upper arm and pinched my flesh until my knees started to buckle. Then, at point-blank range, she shrieked into my ear, "Queen Bees do not destroy evidence at crime scenes!"

"Huh?" What evidence did pictures of Cordy offer? And why was this a crime scene?

"We can't talk here. Let's go." She pulled me across Charleston Avenue, where we were outside of earshot of the crowd but still had a good view of the goings-on.

We didn't talk at first. Sam practiced her deep-breathing exercises, and I thought about heading back to Tinky's for coffee and breakfast.

"First, I apologize for yelling at you. My emotions are running a bit high, what with Connie dead and all."

"Connie is dead?" I asked, hoping I'd heard her wrong.

"Cordy found him stretched out on the sofa, his face pulled back and frozen as if he'd been experiencing excruciating pain. The EMT said it looked like a heart attack, but I can't help but wonder if we have another murder on our hands."

My quick intake of breath sucked saliva into my lungs, and I coughed. Sam slapped me on the back, but I kept coughing. And thinking. Poor Connie.

"Then when I saw you destroying evidence . . ." Sam's voice trailed off.

"Huh?"

"That was Jimmy Kellar. He's the official police photographer. He takes pictures of crime scenes, especially the crowds gathered around watching the cleanup. Sometimes a facial expression or body language can offer a clue. But you destroyed everything."

"Oh." I felt like a deflated balloon. Not just an average birthday balloon, but one of those Macy's Thanksgiving Day Parade ones.

"I thought it went without saying that Queen Bees are not supposed to show emotion, especially frustration or anger."

"Being new to the Queen Bee role and all, I have a lot to learn."

"Yes, you do. And I'm happy to help you. Then you can help me by figuring out which esteemed citizen of Braddocks Beach is a killer."

They say nothing in life is free. I just hoped this returned favor didn't cost me my life.

Chapter Eleven

At the risk of repeating myself, I have no desire to get involved in solving a murder." I crossed my arms in front of me, in a manner daring Sam to defy my wishes.

"At the risk of repeating myself," Sam replied, her hands perched on her hips in an expression of defiance, "there is no danger. We'll ask questions, puzzle things out, and then turn the evidence over to the police for arrest. Not only do you need to shine a positive light back on the Tinsdale name, but now you need to redeem yourself to the police. Trust me, Bennett won't be happy you destroyed an expensive piece of equipment. And he can make your life pretty miserable around here if he wants to."

As if on cue, Chief Bennett's midnight-blue sedan bumped over the curb and settled next to Mystic's truck. Talk about someone who looked ready to kill. I have never seen a face so pinched with anger as the chief's. I slid behind a gigantic oak tree, in case his trigger finger got twitchy, but peeked out enough to watch the rest of the drama unfold.

Mayor Twiddy's white Toyota 4Runner bumped over the curb and pulled up next to Chief Bennett. While the truck rocked to a stop, the mayor flipped open the vanity mirror and checked his hair before opening his door and sliding to the sidewalk.

The two men held a whispered conference before approaching the hum of activity in the front yard. Chief Bennett assumed the stance of authority when he swaggered across the lawn with his hands resting on his gun belt. Mayor Twiddy didn't need a gun. He exuded power and authority naturally.

Sam and I watched the events unfolding from our new position behind Mystic's truck. We were far enough from the activity to not be in the way and yet close enough to observe all the players. My eyes were glued to the scene. The real events were more compelling than any reality TV show I'd ever watched, and trust me, I'd watched a lot.

"Where do you suppose Lorraine is?" Sam whispered out of the corner of her mouth.

As if on cue, a sleek red Mercedes careened around the corner and screeched to a stop behind the 4Runner. Lorraine scrambled out, still wearing the same transparent blouse and red-denim miniskirt from the night before, although now she was barefoot. She raced to the foot of her driveway and pulled up short. With her hands over her mouth, she stared toward her house.

"Where do you suppose she got that car?" Sam didn't seem worried who heard her now.

Puzzled, I asked back, "Isn't it hers?"

"No. She drives a '98 Taurus wagon. Gray."

"That's what she drove off in last night."

"She what?" Sam's voice dropped back down to a stage whisper as she looked around to hear who might have heard what I'd said.

"When I followed her out of your party last night, she took off in this one."

"Which way did she go?"

"Up Charleston. Away from the lake."

"She didn't stop at her house?"

I shook my head.

"Good job, Detective Tinsdale." Sam held out her fist. I bumped hers with mine. I think I may have inadvertently stumbled across our first real clue. I just didn't have a clue what it could possibly mean.

We turned our attention back to the drama unfolding on the front lawn of the Littletons' home. Mayor Twiddy sidled over to Lorraine. I guess he broke the news about Connie's death, because she collapsed into his arms and sobbed uncontrollably. I turned away, having no desire to witness reality this real.

Sam started clapping her hands in slow, short bursts. "Give that lady a Golden Globe."

I turned my head and gave her my most disapproving teacher's look. "What?"

"Lorraine played Lady Macbeth in last spring's production at the Braddocks Beach Little Theater. Very convincingly, I might add. There wasn't a dry eye in the house."

"What're you getting at?"

"I think she's playing the role of grieving widow quite well, don't you? Almost too well? Where's the shock? Where's the disbelief? Where's the numbness?"

Muffled words drifted over the car. I lifted my gaze skyward as if it would enhance my hearing or remove myself from the unspeakable act I was committing. As far as I was concerned, *Thou Shalt Not Eavesdrop* should be the eleventh commandment. It felt very wrong to be listening to a private conversation. But if it helped us find the Braddocks Beach killer, then the ends would justify the means. Or so I rationalized.

"I can't believe it. Connie's gone, gone, gone." Lorraine sobbed. "And I'm expected to plan the funeral?"

"It's okay. It's okay. It's all gonna be okay," Mayor Twiddy cooed. "I'll call Reverend Hammersmith myself. Don't you worry about a thing."

Lorraine's words became muffled as she seemed to bemoan the long list of tasks at hand. Not the least of which, I thought I heard her say, was "a trip to New York for suitable clothes." Now what kind of woman plans a shopping trip when her husband has just died?

"Mayor? Sorry to intrude—" said an unidentified voice.

Sam periscoped her head over the hood of the car and popped back down. "It's Officer Dave," Sam whispered, as if I should be comforted by his presence.

"This isn't a good time," Mayor Twiddy said.

"Chief Bennett told me to ask Mrs. Littleton a few questions."

"Tell Chief Bennett he can eat my shorts. I told you this isn't a good time. Can't you see this woman is completely distraught at just finding out her husband is dead?"

Another mournful wail from Lorraine.

"There's never a good time when death is involved, Mayor. But I must insist. I have only one question."

I couldn't make out what Mayor Twiddy and Lorraine were whispering, but I detected clipped tones and some frustration. The mayor growled and Lorraine's voice rose, shrill and clear, in response. "I have nothing to hide. Go ahead and ask your questions."

"Where were you last night?"

"What do you mean, where was I? I was here, at home with my husband."

"With all due respect, ma'am, none a' the beds have been slept in. None a' the toothbrushes have been used. The bath towels are all dry. And according to my sources, you're wearing the same clothes right now that you had on last night at the Greenes' party. Now, I'll ask one more time, ma'am. Where were you last night?"

More whispered conversations, this time heated and harsh.

"Mrs. Littleton will have no further comment until she has consulted her attorney," Mayor Twiddy said with his voice of authority.

I heard footsteps fading away, and I can only assume Mayor Twiddy escorted Lorraine into the house. Sam turned and slumped down next to me.

"This is going to hamper our investigation. Lorraine's in no condition to be questioned about what Doodles overheard her saying." Sam tapped her fingernail against her teeth and looked at the sky. "Any idea what's the proper amount of time to wait before accusing someone of killing her husband?"

I scratched my head, trying to remember if Madame Rowena ever covered that one.

Chapter Twelve

Woman cannot live on coffee fumes alone. But it seemed as if that's exactly what Sam expected me to do as she propelled me straight past Reba's Pie-ery on our way to Max's office for my ten o'clock appointment. I inhaled deeply, detecting the tantalizing scent of brewing amaretto hazelnut. I wondered if the Geneva Convention forbade countries from withholding coffee from caffeine-addicted prisoners while pumping its intoxicating scent into their dungeons. If not, they should. I know I wouldn't be able to stand up to such torture. I'd spill my guts about anything they wanted to know. Sigh. It's a good thing I'm not a prisoner of war—for more reasons than one.

We'd hung around the Littletons' front yard for another hour or so, but nothing much happened. They'd rolled out Connie's white-sheet-covered body at a quarter past nine. The ragtag crowd began to disperse right after that.

My watch said 9:59. Sam had made it very clear Max didn't tolerate tardiness. Was it my fault she'd made me walk all the way from the Littletons' in shoes that were developed under the motto of "It's better to look good than to feel good"?

We raced up the flight of narrow, creaking steps and propelled our breathless selves past the pebbled-glass door.

"Morning, Merry Sue," Sam said as she shoved me into Max's waiting room.

"Morning, Mrs. Greene, Miss Tinsdale. Max will be with you in a minute. He's been delayed with a phone call this morning. Been on there since I arrived." Merry Sue was wasting her talents as Max's secretary. With her voice, she should consider being a radio host. Or a phone-sex operator.

"Thank you," Sam said as she settled herself onto a blue tweed sofa that looked as tired and saggy as I felt. She patted the cushion next to her. I sat, obedient person that I am.

"Can I get you any coffee or a cold beverage while you wait?" Merry Sue purred.

"Yes, two coffees would be great. Black for me, two creams and one sugar for Miss Tinsdale, please."

"Make mine a double." I hoped Merry Sue heard me. I was in the final stages of caffeine withdrawal, and my head ached something fierce.

"I hope Max is talking to the coroner, getting us some information," Sam said.

"Max did warn us that the officials may be keeping some details confidential until the investigation is complete." I hoped that would be the case today, not wanting the gory details before I'd had some breakfast.

"He'll get us the information we need. Max has a way of making people talk. While you're in with him, I'll pop down to Reba's and see what the word on the street is about Connie's death. When you're done here we'll pop by Veralee's store. Then I think we should stop and pay our respects to Lorraine. I hope that Cordy will be there and can shed some light on her parents' marriage. There is obviously more there than meets the eye. You live two doors down and across the street from someone for thirty-odd years and you think you know them." Sam stopped for a breath. "With your background in science, do you happen to know how long it takes rigor mortis to set in?"

"No, I don't. That's not covered until twelfth-grade biology. My third-grade science lessons don't get much more gruesome than carnivore versus herbivore."

"Then we'll have to make time for some cyber research. Maybe we can estimate Connie's time of death so we can ask around and see who might have been seen around his house at the time of his murder."

"What makes you think it was murder? The EMT said heart attack."

"Because Connie had a medical background and would have called 911 at the first sign, not laid on the sofa and waited to die. We'll use Mizizzy's computer—she has DSL, and we'll get our answers faster. I'll meet you back here in an hour, and we'll head back to the house as soon as we have a chat with Veralee."

"What about Mayor Twiddy? I'm supposed to meet with him at eleven. Maybe I should cancel."

"No, no, no. Queen Bees don't ever cancel without twenty-four hours' notice. It's not polite. We can walk to the municipal center from here, then hit Veralee's, then cyber search. Yeah, that'll work."

My feet lodged a complaint regarding the distance to be covered while wearing heeled shoes, and my stomach protested further. "Can you also squeeze in some food in there somewhere? I'm about to pass out from hunger." That wasn't an exaggeration.

"Of course," Sam said and patted my hand.

Merry Sue returned bearing a Styrofoam cup in each hand. "Here you go."

I took the proffered cup and nodded my thanks. Lifting it to my lips, I took a big gulp. Merry Sue was passing off day-old coffee as fresh, but far be it from me to complain.

Max opened his office door and greeted us with a smile. On the clothing spectrum, he was somewhere between his brand-new suit of yesterday and workout attire of last night. Blue Dockers and a white business shirt, no tie, sleeves rolled to the elbows. He ushered us into the inner sanctum. Sam began her questioning before we'd cleared the threshold. "Any information on Mizizzy's autopsy?"

Max shook his head. "No, not yet. They're keeping a tight lid on this one."

"You'll call me the minute you hear something."

"Sam, have I ever let you down?"

Sam shook her head. "I'll let you two get down to business. Toodles."

The door clicked shut and the room fell silent. Max and I

stared at each other across the big desk like it was the Gunfight at the OK Corral.

I spoke first. "Thanks for coming to my rescue last night. I wasn't looking forward to spending the night on the cot in the jail cell."

"Just doing my j—"

"I don't know any of those women that provided those alibis." I blurted my confession before he finished speaking.

Max stopped stacking papers and looked at me. "You don't?"

I shook my head.

Max huffed through his cheeks. "Sam slipped the papers to me when she walked me to my car last evening, saying she suspected Chief Bennett would arrest you at his first opportunity and that these were proof you didn't kill your aunt. I didn't have time to check their authenticity. We'll keep our fingers crossed that Chief Bennett won't either, or there could be jail time for both of us. Can you give me the names of three actual people who may have seen you that evening?"

I gave him two. Kimmy, the scoliosis-suffering lady whom I run into at the mailbox every evening and hoped would remember seeing me on May 30, and Juan Carlo, my friendly neighborhood convenience-store clerk who'd sold me three boxes of OTC allergy-relief tablets around midnight. Or more like robbed me, at the prices those medicines went for. I couldn't come up with a third. I'd spent most of that weekend suffering in solitude.

"Anything else that could result in litigation I need to be aware of? I don't like to be blindsided." He smiled, as if it were a joke. Too bad it wasn't.

I shifted in my seat. "You might be getting a call from a police photographer. I threw his camera under a fire truck this morning. He threatened legal action."

Max threw his head back and laughed.

"I'm serious."

He stopped midchuckle and stared at me. He seemed to be struggling against the urge to roll his eyes back in his head. I imagine he was wishing he wasn't my attorney right about now.

"How much do you suppose the equipment was worth?" he asked.

"It had a very big lens and looked kind of expensive. I'm more of a disposable-camera kind of gal, so I wouldn't dare to guess."

Max made a few notes on a legal pad and then laid his pen down, leaned back in his chair, and folded his hands across his stomach. "I didn't realize a penchant for trouble was a genetic trait. You are very much like your aunt." Max shifted in his seat, the leather squawking in protest. "You'll do fine in this town. Which brings me to the last few details of the will."

"I promise not to faint today."

Max smiled. "I imagine it's a bit overwhelming. But we covered most of it yesterday. As I said before, the terms of the will require that you reside within the city limits of Braddocks Beach for five years. You can go as far as Cleveland, as your aunt realized the cultural things offered there might be of interest to you, and shopping up Medina way and such. But every night you must be tucked into bed here in town. There's a method to Isabel's madness. She felt confident that once you learned about your heritage and learned to love the town as we all do, that you'd live the rest of your life here of your own free will."

"No weekend retreats?"

Max shook his head.

"Time off for good behavior?"

Max shook his head again.

My shoulders slumped. Traveling was in my soul. Could I forsake it for five long years? "And after five years, if I don't like it?"

"Then you sell the real estate to the highest bidder, take the money, and ride off into the sunset."

"Is it all or nothing?" Butterflies started fluttering in the pit of my stomach and quickly morphed into tiny men with jackhammers.

"Yup. If you leave town on day, let's see"—he punched the buttons on a calculator and then held it up to read the display—

"one thousand eight hundred and fifty-four, you leave with nothing. On the first day of your sixth year, the money is yours. We started counting yesterday at two."

"So I could maybe stick around for a month or two, see how it goes, then make my commitment?"

"The only commitment is to you. There is no contract to sign. You don't owe anything to anybody."

Five years. Five springs, five summers, five falls I could probably endure. But five winters? I'd need a new coat. A heavy parka. Warm boots. Flannel-lined jeans. Electric blanket. Come to think of it, I'd need a lot of things. My Queen Bee uniform had already set me back a couple of hundred. And what about entertainment? And food! "What about living expenses? I'd have to give up my teaching career," I blurted, not bothering to disguise my desperation.

"Upkeep of the house and grounds will be provided from the estate, as well as utilities."

"What about everything else? Health insurance? Car insurance? Car repairs, even?" I loved Bessie, but she was high maintenance.

"What do you live on now?"

"My teaching salary. But Sam says I won't have time to work, what with being the Queen Bee and all."

"Certainly you have some savings."

"Um. Well. My investments aren't exactly liquid."

"Not a problem. We can arrange a loan against them. What kind? Long-term CDs? Municipal bonds? Whole life insurance?" He poised his pen above his tablet of paper.

How to explain this. "I've invested everything I've earned in memories."

Max gave me a blank stare.

It's a tough concept, but I tried to explain it. "My income covers the basic necessities of life. Food, clothing, shelter, and travel. As soon as I get a few dollars saved, I book another trip. The cruise to Alaska, which leaves in thirteen days, took all my savings. It's too late to get a refund."

I waited for Max's reaction. I wasn't sure the information

was computing in his brain. The phone rang at Merry Sue's desk. A car honked on the street below. The poker-playing dogs smirked at me from their two-dimensional game table behind Max's head. My stomach's growl echoed throughout the room.

"Memories are great for warming the soul, but they don't go far in putting food on the table," Max said. He understood. At least I thought he did. Until he sighed again. A great big long sigh of resignation. Poor Max. Poor me.

Max drummed his pen against the paper. "I think we can interpret the terms of the will to cover all your basic living expenses—food, clothing and shelter, and other necessities— within reason, of course. But no travel."

"Understood." I relaxed. I'd have plenty of time, and money, to see the world once my sentence had been served. In the meantime, I was going to be a kept woman. With Max controlling the purse strings. That thought did not rest easy on my conscience. "And legal expenses?" At the rate I was going, they could become significant.

"The trustee fees will come out of the proceeds, of course. We'll work something out with the rest."

The office door banged opened and Merry Sue raced in. "Connie Littleton is dead!"

I heard a thump and looked to find Max had fallen out of his chair. Merry Sue and I raced around the desk to find him flat on his back, staring at the ceiling.

Between Merry Sue and me, we got Max back into his big chair. I fanned him with his legal pad while Merry Sue poured a glass of water from the pitcher on the credenza.

"I don't believe it. Not Connie. Please not Connie," Max moaned.

Sam appeared behind me, her gaze darting around as she assessed the situation. "He just hear the bad news?"

I nodded.

"I think this calls for something a little stronger than wind and water. Merry Sue, do you have a bottle of Scotch around here somewhere?" Sam asked.

"Something came in one of Veralee's Christmas baskets. I think it's here somewhere."

"Could you find it, please?"

Merry Sue disappeared in the blink of an eye. I waited for my assignment, needing to do more than fan cool air on Max's bloodless face.

"Max. Max. Listen to me," Sam said. "I have some questions to ask you. Do you know of any reason someone would murder Connie?"

Max turned his glazed-over eyes in Sam's direction. "It's that damn secret. I'm sure of it."

"What secret?" Sam and I asked in unison. Could this secret be the same secret project Connie and Aunt Izzy had been working on? Or could there be more than one secret tucked behind the white picket fences of this small town?

"I don't know. I don't know. I don't know," Max mumbled and moaned.

Sam stopped Max's broken record with a not-exactly-gentle pat to his cheek. His head stilled and his gaze focused on a picture of him and Connie holding a three-foot catfish between them.

Max's words came out in a whisper. "He and Miss Izzy were working on some secret project. They wouldn't give me any details. None. Just said I'd see soon enough."

"'Three can keep a secret if two are dead,'" I re-quoted what he'd said to me last night.

"I'd overheard your conversation with Connie and was jealous he was going to tell you his secret. You, a complete stranger, and me his most trusted friend." Max balled his hands into fists and pounded them on the arms of his chair.

"Did Connie act like he thought he was in danger?" Sam hitched her hip on Max's desk and leaned in closer.

Max shook his head.

"Ever say that he thought Mizizzy was murdered because of it?"

Max shook his head.

Merry Sue returned carrying a silver tray displaying a bottle of Dewar's and four cut-glass tumblers. She poured three fingers in each and handed the glasses around. When Sam and I refused, she gave one to Max and lifted the other in a toast, then slogged back the contents in one glug. Max did the same. Glasses three and four were dispatched by them with an equally efficient motion.

Sam reached for the bottle and poured another round.

Merry Sue lifted her glass in salute and then turned and stumbled out of the room. Sam settled her hip on Max's desk and stared into his eyes. "Do you think Lorraine could have killed Connie?"

"Yeah, if she found out about—" Max cut himself off. "Sorry, attorney-client privilege." Max sat silently, tossing back tumbler after tumbler of Dewar's.

We sat silently waiting for the alcohol to kick in with the hope he'd become more loquacious when under the influence.

After the second chorus of "Danny Boy," we gave up and left.

Chapter Thirteen

Are you thinking what I'm thinking?" Sam asked as we exited the dimness of Flossie's Pharmacy. I squinted against the sunlight of a glorious summer's morn. The three Fig Newtons I'd stuffed in my mouth prevented me from answering, but I figured it was a rhetorical question, anyway. I was right.

"I think Lorraine killed both Connie and Mizizzy."

I swallowed the large lump of fruit and cake and felt my blood sugar levels surge upward to a respectable level. "We don't have any proof that Connie died of anything other than a heart attack."

"I have all the proof I need right here." Sam tapped her fingers against her solar plexus. "A gut feeling. No doubt in my mind. He was healthy as a horse. A heart attack on the one night Lorraine doesn't spend at home? I don't believe in coincidences. We need to kick our question asking up a notch and find this killer. Be glad Connie didn't share the secret with you, or the killer might be gunning after you at this very second."

Me? On a killer's next-to-splatter-her-brains-all-over-the-sidewalk list? I officially felt the bejesus scared out of me. My involuntary muscles stopped functioning, and I had to tell my lungs to breath and my heart to beat. Enough of playing Bess Marvin to Sam's Nancy Drew. I wanted out. "Here's an idea," I said, my voice sounding much calmer than I felt. "Let's let the police do their job."

"Really, Ellery. What part of 'Chief Bennett is a bumbling idiot' don't you get? You're his number-one suspect in Mizizzy's murder, and I wouldn't be at all surprised if he has you on the top of the list for Connie's—peace be with him—also. My motivation is not just to protect the Tinsdale name, but to keep you out of jail. You know what they'd do to a cream puff like you in the big house?"

Dead or in jail. Not good options. *Breathe in. Breathe out,* I told my lungs.

"Let's go."

What choice did I have? Really?

First stop on our Talk, Look, and Listen Tour was City Hall.

The four-story, three-winged brick building could have been modeled after a Norman Rockwell print. A sweeping expanse of statuesque oak trees dotting a lush green lawn led up to the grand pillared entrance. A sign indicated the library to the left, the police station to the right, and city offices in the middle.

"Let me do the talking with Zanna." Sam tapped her foot while waiting for the elevator to drop to our level.

"Who's Zanna? I thought we were here to see Mayor Twiddy."

"Susanna, or Zanna for short, is the city treasurer and Lorraine's best friend. She works here and might know something."

A ding announced the elevator's arrival. The doors slid open with a soft swish, exposing an empty car. We stepped in and they swished closed behind us.

"Zanna can be a bit protective of Lorraine. In fact, now that I think about it, she might not even be here. She may be over at Lorraine's. This is all just such a shock. I'm not thinking clearly."

"Plus it's Saturday," I offered helpfully.

"By mayoral decree, the work week for all city employees is Tuesday through Saturday. Most of the citizens who work Monday through Friday conduct their business on Saturday, so it's one of the busiest days here."

The elevator whooshed to a halt, and the doors slid open. Sam preceded me into a large, open-aired office humming with activity. Decorated in muted shades of gray and mauve and portioned off with portable walls, it was a Dilbert cartoon in the making. A perky receptionist sat perched behind a crescent-moon desk.

"Hi, Precious. Is Ms. Wilson in, please?" Sam asked.

"I'll check her availability, Mrs. Greene. If you and Miss Tinsdale would like to take a seat." Precious pointed to small seating group.

We made ourselves as comfortable as possible on two side chairs that were built for form, not function. Sam flipped through a glossy magazine, but unless she'd graduated summa cum laude from an Evelyn Woods Speed Reading class, she wasn't reading, only glancing at the pictures. Between quick peeks to scan the room, that is. "I think we're in luck," she mumbled under her breath. "I just saw Zanna buzz around the corner."

A moment later, Precious told us we could go on back to Zanna's office.

Back we went, Sam leading in the manner of a conditioned mouse heading through the maze toward the cheese. Reaching the farthest corner of the building, we walked into a fully enclosed office and were greeted by a short woman who looked like she exercised about as much as I did.

"Thanks so much for seeing us," Sam said. "You remember Ellery from the party last night."

And I remembered Zanna, who couldn't sing "Tomorrow" to save her life. Today she'd squeezed her pleasant plumpness into a tailored emerald-green suit. Her hair was overgrown, overteased, and overcolored to an unnatural shade of burgundy. Her expression made me wonder if she'd eaten a bad burrito for breakfast.

Zanna took her place behind her desk and motioned for us to take a seat.

"Oh no, we're on our way to meet Mayor Twiddy," Sam said. "As long as we were in the building, I thought we'd just stop by to see if there's anything we could do for Lorraine. I'm assuming you'll be helping coordinate the events?"

Zanna nodded, her expression slipping from a grimace to a frown. "I'm heading that way as soon as I tie up a few things here."

I felt the tingling of an impending sneeze and wriggled my nose to stave it off.

"Please put the Charleston Avenue contingent down for the post-funeral repast. I'll rally the troops. They put on such a fabulous spread for Mizizzy."

"I'll make sure the family knows."

I sneezed. A diminutive sneeze, and nobody seemed to notice.

"Thank you. Such a tragedy," Sam said in hushed tones. "Have you spoken with Lorraine yet?"

"No. Cordy called me with the news about an hour ago. She said Lorraine ran out of the house. Said she couldn't stand being in the same place where Connie bit the biscuit."

Sam gasped. "Lorraine said that?"

"Don't be daft. She wasn't that delicate." Zanna threw back her head and cackled like a rooster.

I wiggled my fingers in my ear, wondering if I'd just heard what I'd heard. It didn't seem right for the poster child for wedded bliss to be so callous about the passing of her husband. But then, she could already be in the first, or was it second, stage of grief: anger. I sneezed again, this time a bit louder and a bit juicier. I needed a tissue.

"God bless you," Sam said, then turned back to Zanna. "Does anyone know where Lorraine is?"

"Took off in that new car of hers, I heard."

"I can't believe that Connie sprang for such an extravagance."

"He didn't."

"Oh?"

"Lorraine won it in a contest."

I listened to the verbal ping-pong match while glancing around the room for the source of the nose irritant. No flowers, no perfume scents. Not too much dust, at least not more than I was used to living with at home. Maybe it was Zanna's polyester.

"I'm surprised there wasn't more hoopla. Mystic lives for stories like that." Sam seemed to be speaking her thoughts aloud, and she seemed irritated that something had occurred in this town that she hadn't been informed of.

"You know Lorraine wouldn't give Mystic a scoop of dog poop."

Sam pursed her lips.

"Not since that—"

The intercom buzzed, interrupting Zanna's explanation. A hoarse voice said, "Mrs. Littleton is on the phone. She said it's urgent."

The Braddocks Beach city treasurer pushed a button and lifted the receiver to her ear. "Lorraine? I'm so sorry. Yes. Cordy called me." Zanna waved her fingers at us in an irritated gesture of farewell, then sat down and propped her forehead in the *V* of her hand.

I started for the door. Sam laid a restraining hand on my arm and I paused. I'm not sure it's eavesdropping if you're not hiding. Still, it felt wrong.

My nose tickled again. I pinched it shut, held my breath, and listened to one side of the phone conversation.

"Where are you? With whom? Why? I don't think that's a great idea. Why don't you come stay with me? I'll make up the guest room. We'll make plans . . . I know it's hard . . . We'll get through this . . . That's what friends are for . . . Tell you what, I'll make a batch of Goombay Smashes. We haven't had one since you joined AA."

I knew from personal experience (three weeks on Bimini— gawd, what a vacation that had been) that the potent combination of pineapple and orange juices; coconut cream; light, dark, and coconut rums; and triple sec was not for the faint of heart. And certainly not for someone with a drinking problem.

"No." Zanna continued talking into the receiver, her thumb and middle finger massaging the area at her scalp line. "I thought you told me Cordy was the executrix. Uh-huh. Well, when Mom died it took a few months. We need to get through the funeral first, and then we'll worry about money. Who's taking care of the arrangements? Really? I would have thought Reverend Hammersmith—"

I lost the battle with the sneeze. And it was a big one. A great big *ha-ha-ha-CHOO!* that drew Zanna's head up with a snap. The anger in her eyes made it very clear she didn't appreciate Sam and me standing in the doorway, hanging on her every word.

"Excuse me one minute, Lorraine." Small dots of red appeared on Zanna's cheeks. She lifted her mouth away from the mouthpiece and spoke to us in a no-nonsense voice. "If you'll excuse me, this is a private conversation."

"Of course, Zanna," Sam explained. "I'm just waiting for you to confirm with Lorraine about the arrangements for after the funeral and then I'll give the green light to the food committee." Sam pointed her French-tipped fingernail toward the phone and nodded her head as if to say, "Go ahead, ask her, and we'll be on our way."

I felt another sneeze coming on, put a finger under my nose, and looked up at the lights in my tried-and-true method of staving off sneezes. No luck. Another sneeze that could blow the roof off the place erupted from me.

Just as I was about to wipe my nose on the sleeve of my blouse (for lack of any tissues available), Sam whipped a blue-lace-edged handkerchief from the pocket of her dress and stuffed it in my hand. I missed the rest of the conversation as I stepped out to the hallway to blow my nose. Although it felt wrong doing so into such a dainty piece of fabric, I blew, then sneezed again, and again, and again. The next thing I knew, Sam brushed past me and headed back through the maze of cubicles. I followed, blowing and sneezing in her tsk-tsking wake.

"Did you hear all that?" Sam whispered as we made our way to the elevator.

"Hear what?"

"Our sleuthing paid off."

The elevator car arrived and we stepped on. "How so?" I asked.

"We found out that Cordy is executrix."

That didn't seem unusual to me.

"Lorraine is already worried about the money."

I didn't know Lorraine well enough to comment on that.

"Somebody other than Reverend Hammersmith is taking care of the arrangements."

That only raised a bigger question in my mind. If not the reverend, then who?

"And, I need a drum roll here, that Lorraine won that car in a contest."

Funny, out of all that, Sam thought the car was the most significant piece of information.

The doors opened onto the third floor. We stepped into a space with the same cubicle plan, color scheme, and receptionist station as the floor below, only this perky young girl had hair twisted into two Heidi-like braids.

"Good morning, Snippy. Miss Tinsdale and I are here for an eleven o'clock appointment with Mayor Twiddy." Sam stepped up to the desk. "Ellery, I'd like you to meet Snippy, who'll be leaving for journalism school at the end of the summer."

Snippy stood and offered her hand. "Nice to meet you, Miss Tinsdale."

"You too." I nodded.

"I'm sorry you've wasted your time coming up here," Snippy said. "If your appointment had been on the calendar I would have called you. The mayor is over at the Littletons'. Too sad, all that, huh? You heard?"

"No. What's happened?" Sam did her innocent thing again.

"Connie Littleton is dead." Snippy seemed happy to be the bearer of sad news.

Sam gasped. When I felt an elbow to my ribs, I gasped too. "How?" I think I sounded convincing.

"Murdered!"

This time our joint surprise was genuine.

"A bloody duel, I heard, over a woman, no less!" The receptionist proceeded to give us a long, overly embellished tale of romantic entanglements, disturbing jealousies, and blackmail—without specific names. I couldn't help but think Snippy was missing her calling; she should be a romance writer, not a journalist.

With the story over, and my tour of the city postponed indefinitely, Sam and I returned to the elevator and stood silently until we were safely behind closed doors and on our way down. "Well, partner, we definitely have got ourselves another murder to solve." The excitement in Sam's voice scared me.

"Sam, you can't believe a word of what that girl said."

"And why not?"

"Because you heard from Cordy herself that there was no blood."

"I know that."

"And certainly no duel."

"I know that."

"The EMT said it was a heart attack."

"I know that. But how do you know the killer didn't just make it look like a heart attack? Hmm? And while I agree that the local gossip lines do tend to embellish every story to epic proportions, we can't rule out lust, greed, or jealousy as motives. Snippy has given us an outline to work with. We just have to fill in a few names."

And keep our names out of it.

I could really go for a double Goombay Smash right now.

Chapter Fourteen

If not with alcohol, then I'd just have to resort to calming my frazzled nerves with fudge. Mountains of it. My gaze scanned across the white-flag labels positioned on the top of each fudgy mountain: chocolate amaretto swirl, chocolate butter-finger, chocolate caramel pecan, chocolate peanut butter cup, deep chocolate, deep chocolate walnut, maple walnut, mochacchino chip, peanut butter, penuche, vanilla, vanilla caramel, vanilla cherry.

Hansel and Gretel's Gifts and Goodies was officially my favorite place on earth.

"Let me do the talking," Sam said under her breath as we waited for our turn to speak with Veralee Leinhart, the proprietress, whose husband played poker with the town coroner.

A woman's head popped over the top of the fudge case. I recognized her immediately as the shaggy-banged woman I'd name-associated with a sheepdog. Today she wore a light blue pinafore that reminded me of Dorothy in *The Wizard of Oz*.

"Hello, Veralee. Ellery, you remember Veralee Leinhart from last night's potluck, don't you?"

"Yes." I smiled. I so wanted to take a pair of scissors to those straggles of brown hair that fell to midcheek. I caught a glimpse of soft gray eyes when she puffed the hair off her face, only to have it fall back in a curtain of privacy. "Nice to see you again. What a wonderful store you have here."

Veralee puffed her bangs again. "Thank you. I've got some great ideas for expansion. I'd like to do more with wines and crackers and other snack foods to flesh out the gift baskets some, but that stinkpot next door is nothing but talk when it

88

comes to selling out and retiring to Florida. Morty's been promising me for three years now. I mean, he averages two, maybe three customers per week. That's not a business; it's a hobby. Who's he fooling?"

I heard the *ka-ching* of an old-fashioned cash register in the distance. Business seemed to be booming in here. I had no doubt in my mind I would be contributing to its success over the next five years.

"Can I help you ladies with anything this afternoon? A sample of fudge, perhaps?"

"That—" I intended to finish with "—would be wonderful," but Sam interrupted me.

"No, thanks just the same. It smells delicious as always, but we're here on official business."

"Do you need a party catered?" Veralee asked, an extra-hearty puff of her bangs revealing an eager gaze dashing between Sam and me.

"Not at the moment. Our official business today is to inform you that Ellery has inherited all of her aunt's real estate holdings." Sam nodded in my direction.

That drew a sharp intake of breath from both Veralee and me.

"You . . . you . . . you mean that she, I mean you, Miss Tinsdale, own this strip of stores?" Veralee's hands parted the curtain of bangs and her gray eyes peered at me like a hopeful puppy.

I blinked and looked at Sam. I didn't have a clue what I owned. Technically, I didn't own anything yet. And wouldn't for some time. If ever. I guess I hadn't made that part clear to Sam, and now didn't seem the time to bring up that detail.

"Yes," Sam answered for me. "And Morty has already approached Max regarding the termination of his lease. It runs through next April, but he might be interested in heading south before the snow flies. As early as September. Perhaps something can be worked out to enable you to expand. And . . ." Sam glanced around as if to make sure nobody was eavesdropping, and then leaned closer to the counter. ". . . Miss Tinsdale might even be interested in *selling* the property." The lie seemed to roll off Sam's tongue like butter off hot corn bread.

With her bangs still tugged out of her face, Veralee's eyes darted to the wall, and I imagined she was imagining it gone and her store overflowing into the new space.

"Of course," Sam continued, "Mizizzy's will can't be executed until the cause of death is official. And the murderer found. I don't suppose Rob has mentioned Bernard saying anything over the poker table?"

"No, not that I can remember. I'll certainly ask him, though. In fact, I'll call him right now. Won't take but a moment." She disappeared through the chintz curtains hanging behind the cash register at the back of the store.

"I can't believe you told her I'd sell all this," I hissed at Sam. "That's an outright lie."

"Relax. Morty spoke to Mizizzy last March about closing his shop in September. Seems sports memorabilia has gone cyber, and his store can't compete with the Internet. He asked that she not say anything to Veralee. Seems she stops by his store on a regular basis, gift basket in hand, and subtly drops hints that he should close his shop and retire somewhere warm. He figures as soon as he agrees to that, no more baskets. So, no harm, no foul, as they say, right?" Sam shrugged her shoulders with Shirley Temple innocence.

"But you're bargaining away Morty's secret for information on Aunt Izzy's death."

"Do you have a better idea?"

I did not.

The Sheepdog came scurrying back, motioning us to meet her at the end of the display cases. We huddled our three heads together while Veralee whispered the disturbing news. "Bernard said that Ms. Tinsdale died of severe head trauma. Very bloody and brutal."

I laid my forearm on the cool metal edge of the fudge display case.

"Basically, her head was bashed in and her brains splattered all over the floor of the watchtower."

"Which side?"

"Of the watchtower?"

"No. Which side of her face?"

"The right side, I think. Yeah, I'm pretty sure."

Too much detail. I laid my head against the back of my hand, worrying that my legs wouldn't support me much longer.

"They have yet to identify the murder weapon. Bigger than a baseball bat, Bernard said, but that's not for sure yet."

Poor Aunt Izzy. What could she have done to deserve such brutality?

"The police are investigating, of course, but keeping the autopsy under wraps in hopes of using some of the details to trip up the killer. I hope you understand I'm breaking a sacred poker trust by telling you this."

"And we appreciate it." Sam grasped Veralee's hands in her own. "I think this news has upset Ellery. I need to get her home now. We'll stop by in the next few weeks and discuss business."

More whispers that I couldn't comprehend. I was too busy focusing on the gruesome images of Aunt Izzy's last moments on earth.

The fresh air helped ease my distress. Marginally. The walk home was silent. And slow. The news seemed to have taken the wind out of Sam's sails too.

"So, I was wrong," Sam said as we hauled ourselves up the steps of Aunt Izzy's front porch.

"How so?"

"It wasn't a gun. That could have been an accident, or a case of mistaken identity, or a moment of bad judgment or panic on the killer's part. Beating someone until their brains ooze out takes a really violent person hell-bent on making sure the victim is good and dead."

That didn't bear thinking about, Not now. Not ever. I blocked the whole thing from my mind. Denial is my most exercised defense mechanism.

Back at the house, we stepped into the foyer. It felt like years, not mere hours, since we'd left for our morning breakfast appointment with Mystic. I glanced at the glass-domed anniversary clock on the mantel in the parlor. Its spinning pendulum twirled the seconds away. Bessie and I had rolled into Braddocks Beach exactly twenty-four hours ago. At that point, Aunt Izzy had merely been dead. Now she'd been brutally murdered. And Connie Littleton too. Maybe.

"You up for a little Web surfing?"

Physically, mentally, and emotionally drained, about the only thing I was up for was a little summer's nap. "No rest for the weary, I guess."

"And the righteous don't need any," Sam said.

I couldn't agree less.

Chapter Fifteen

We've got our work cut out for us," Sam said. "Let's get busy. I'll go fire up Mizizzy's computer. Why don't you scrounge around in the pantry and see what you can find? I'm feeling a bit peckish."

The thought of food had me skipping down a hallway whose walls had Aunt Izzy's life laid out in eight-by-ten glossies. One particular photo caught my eye. Aunt Izzy couldn't have been more than two years old. A teenage boy, presumably my father, was on his knees, holding two ice cream cones. One for his baby sister to lick, the other held out for a dog to enjoy. Aunt Izzy would have been about six when my dad left town, and yet she'd stayed loyal to him all these years. Loyal enough to leave everything to me, a stranger. I felt such sorrow that I hadn't had an opportunity to meet her.

"Hurry up, Ellery. I think I found something," Sam called from upstairs.

I dropped my arms, which I hadn't realized I'd wrapped around my midsection, and headed back for the kitchen. The best way I could repay Aunt Izzy would be to bring her killer to justice. And I couldn't do that on an empty stomach.

The pantry held a treasure trove of snacks. My gaze flitted from cereal shelf to canned vegetables shelf to crunchy snacks shelf and then, lo and behold, a dessert shelf. Lined up in alphabetical order was the entire line of Pepperidge Farm Milano cookies: Double Chocolate, Milk Chocolate, Mint, Orange, and Raspberry. I gasped with the realization that Aunt Izzy was alive. Not "alive" in the physical sense, in that she'd been pirated away in the witness protection program somewhere, and another woman's face had been beaten beyond recognition, or even the paranormal sense in that her spirit would be dragging chains down the stairs or moaning at all hours of the night. I meant *alive* in that she was not a glossy photograph, but a real flesh-and-blood woman who had lived and breathed and loved and shared her DNA. With me.

We had the same cookie-loving gene.

I tore into the bag of Orange Milanos, crunching through a stack of them the way some people eat Pringles potato chips. While chewing, I scanned the room for other clues to Aunt Izzy's character. She'd died unexpectedly ten days ago, and yet not one thing was out of place in her kitchen. Not so much as a dishtowel tossed onto the counter. No morning coffee mug in the sink. No peaches or bananas ripening on the counter. We didn't share that cleanliness gene. I preferred clutter and a reluctant biannual straightening.

"Ellery, are you coming up here or not?" Sam's excited voice drifted from somewhere above me.

"Be right there." The bag of cookies was almost gone, and Sam didn't strike me as a Milano-cookie girl anyway. Deep in the bowels of the pantry, tucked behind the Fritos and fried pork rinds, I found a can of bacon-flavored Cheez Whiz. Not exactly baby Gouda, but it would jazz up the water crackers. I rounded out the midday snack with cold sodas. With food and drinks cradled in my arms, I headed upstairs.

During my tour yesterday, I'd dubbed the first floor the "museum," as it was filled to the point of being cluttered with antiques. Although I'm no expert, I suspected every last doily dated back to the day the house had been built, in 1879—or so proclaimed the plaque by the front door. The only nod to modernization was the kitchen, comparatively speaking, in that it had a stove and plumbing that wouldn't have been part of the original plans, but it was, at pre-1960s, still antique by my standards.

The second floor was a bit more contemporary and a lot more comfortable. The furniture was dated and dented, but the fabrics were strictly twenty-first-century Bed Bath & Beyond. I had no recollection of seeing a computer, or even a piece of furniture that could hide one, anywhere in the house. I poked my nose into every room as creaking floorboards marked my progress down the hall.

"Hurry up. I've found a great site on death that explains everything."

Even though I was on the second floor, Sam's voice still seemed to come from above. The door to the attic gaped open and harsh, fluorescent light filtered down. I hadn't given a second thought to the rickety stairs I'd discovered yesterday.

The passageway was tight, and I had to turn sideways to fit around the 180-degree turn halfway up the white wainscoted stairway. I stepped into a sleek, twenty-first-century office space, defined by chrome and glass and all things technological. And the biggest computer screen I'd ever seen. Good for Aunt Izzy for keeping on the cutting edge of things.

"Pull up a chair," Sam said. "I'll give you a crash lesson on death and rigor mortis."

With no La-Z-Boy in sight, I grabbed a white leather highbacked seat, complete with headrest. It looked more like something you lie in when a dentist cleans your teeth than a desk chair.

"It's amazing the information available with the click of a mouse. The Internet is an amazing thing. An entire Web site devoted to dead bodies. Listen to what I found. 'Rigor mortis is the state a body reaches when the oxygen supply to the muscles ceases but the cells continue to respire anaerobically, which means without oxygen. This causes lactic acid to build up, which affects the muscles, causing stiffening, termed rigor mortis. Bodies become stiff after about three hours and remain that way for around thirty-six hours. Rigor mortis ceases as the body cells die, enzymes are released, and the cells decompose.' Watch this." Sam double-clicked her way through the slide show of the stages of pig decomposition.

I couldn't watch. Instead, I focused my gaze on the flamingo

Beanie Baby perched atop the computer screen, trying my very hardest *not* to look. My mind wandered, rehashing the scant bit of information we knew about Connie's death.

"Connie died sometime in the wee hours of the morning," I said, not realizing I'd deduced that until the words came out of my mouth.

Sam's head swiveled from the computer screen to me at that comment. "How do you figure that?"

"After you consoled Cordy this morning, you said she said she'd found him, and his face seemed frozen in pain. Sounds like rigor mortis had set in. She found him sometime after seven, while we were eating breakfast. He must have been dead at least three hours. He was very much alive at nine thirty last night, so I'd say time of death was sometime between ten last night and three this morning."

"I'm impressed."

I smiled and reclined back in the chair. I had to admit, I was pretty impressed myself.

"So, what's next?" Sam asked.

Now that my belly was full of cookies, I found it very difficult to focus on anything other than a siesta. "A nap?"

Sam ignored my suggestion. "I think it's time we paid our condolences to the grieving widow."

"What if she's not home?" I asked, not bothering to disguise the hopeful note in my voice.

"It's proper etiquette for the newly bereaved to make themselves available to receive visitors. Trust me when I say Lorraine will be holding court. She may have run off at first, but protocol has visitors arriving within six hours of sad news. Besides, we need to find out when the services will be held so we can begin coordinating the dinner." Sam executed a series of mouse clicks and the computer sang its good-night song. "What's your signature dish?" She was out of her chair and halfway down the stairs.

"My what?" I hauled my tired body up and followed.

"Your signature dish. The one you're renowned for taking to potluck events."

"Oh. I usually take a Piggly Wiggly deli platter. Genoa salami and pepper jack cheese."

Sam seemed to find that funny. When the chuckles abated, she said, "No, seriously. There's got to be something that you make and everyone asks for the recipe and you decline to give away your culinary secrets."

I thought about that as we descended the second set of stairs. "One time I tried a recipe off the Internet where you take a tube of sugar cookie dough and spread it on a pie pan and bake it, then top it with strawberry Cool Whip and fresh strawberries. Everyone raved about it."

"That's interesting, but not quite the wow factor expected from a Queen Bee. Don't worry, we'll find something."

I hesitated to tell her that was the most gourmet dish I'd ever attempted. Another failing in my genetic code.

We crossed Charleston Avenue and made our way along the shady side of the street toward the Littletons' house. Lorraine's shiny new sports car sat at the top of her circular driveway, gleaming like a blinking beacon. Both doors stood open, the way they do on the showroom floor, only no one stood around salivating over the interior's bling.

"Why won't Lorraine give Mystic the story?" Zanna had mentioned something to that effect.

"About five years ago, Lorraine had a complete body overhaul. Nips and tucks, a little more here and a little less there. Went all the way to Hollywood to use some surgeon to the stars. Mystic had some connection to the guy and, through a series of bizarre coincidences, she found out about it. The story landed on the front page of the Tri-B the very day Lorraine returned from a six-week cruise." Sam air-quoted the word *cruise*. "Lorraine was furious. She'd hoped to surprise everyone. The effect was lost because after they'd read about it they raced, en masse, to her house. They'd caught her in curlers and without makeup to cover the scars. So, Lorraine's big bang was little more than a whistle in a category-four hurricane. Mystic and Lorraine haven't spoken since. In fact, Lorraine has been known to snub her when they attend AA meetings together. It's just poor manners, and Lorraine should know better."

We trudged up the steps. Sam pulled the screen door open and walked right into the house as if she owned the place. What could I do but follow?

A tall, thin-faced, dour-looking man dressed in black Dockers and a faded yellow polo shirt (that I suspected had been lemon-colored in a previous life) greeted us in the grand foyer.

"Vice Mayor Applewhite, nice to see you. May I introduce Ellery Tinsdale? Ellery, this is our esteemed vice mayor." We shook hands and exchanged pleasantries.

"Is Lorraine receiving this afternoon?" Sam asked.

"She's with Reverend Hammersmith and Mayor Twiddy at the moment. There are many arrangements to be made. I'm sure you understand." He spoke without emotion.

Sam and I nodded our heads solemnly.

"Mrs. Littleton has asked me to request people return this evening. A potluck affair."

"I'd better get cooking then. Ellery will be presenting her signature dish."

My hand flew out and smacked Sam in the bicep.

Sam threw me a Queen-Bees-do-not-smack-people look, then turned her attention to Applewhite. "I'm coordinating the dinner afterward. I'm expecting at least two hundred, don't you think? Connie didn't know a stranger, and they'll all want to pay their respects. The sooner I can get to planning, the better. I was hoping to speak with Lorraine regarding the dates."

"Tuesday afternoon is what I've been told," Applewhite said solemnly.

Sam laid a hand against her throat. "So soon? Does that give them time to perform the autopsy?"

"It is my understanding there will be no autopsy. Connie had a weak heart and died of a heart attack."

"I thought all deaths required an autopsy . . ." Sam let her voice trail off.

"Only if the police deem the death suspicious, or the family requests it. Neither of those apply in this instance."

Sam maintained her gracious smile, but her clipped voice made it clear she wasn't pleased with this news. "Well, then, we'll just come back this evening. Please express our deepest condolences to Lorraine and Cordy for us, won't you?"

We'd barely hit the sidewalk before Sam grabbed me by the elbow and pulled me up short. "Did you hear that?"

"Hear what?"

"They're not going to perform an autopsy! I can't believe it. How will we ever know if he was murdered?"

I didn't have an answer to that. I'm not sure Sam expected one.

"Okay, I have a plan," she said.

By the glimmer in Sam's eye, I had the uneasy feeling that her plan involved something illegal, immoral, or, at the least, unethical.

And I'd already used my get-out-of-jail-free card.

Chapter Sixteen

Sam's plan involved getting out of town. Nothing immoral or unethical about that, and only borderline illegal in that she urged me to push Bessie to her age-hampered limits.

Sam remained uncharacteristically silent, hunkered down in the passenger seat as we sped past the lush green hills and valleys of central Ohio. The scratch of her felt-tip pen against her notepad reminded me of fingernails on a chalkboard. To drown out the noise, I tapped Bessie's radio button and searched for any song that wasn't staticky or screamy, settling on Billy Joel's "Piano Man." Ahh, music for the soul.

"Will you please turn that racket off? Can't you see I'm trying to think?"

I complied, but not without a grunt of annoyance.

"Sorry, I didn't mean to snap. But this needs to be just right. You're going to get only one crack at it."

"Me? What exactly will I be taking a crack at?" My concerns over immoral or unethical deeds bubbled forth once more.

"A phone call to the SBI."

"I hope you're referring to the Stampeding Buffalo Insurgency or something?"

"State Bureau of Investigation."

Exactly what I'd hoped *not* to hear.

"Have you seen a pay phone yet?" she asked.

"I haven't seen a pay phone in five years. They went the way of the dodo bird when cell phones became smaller than a breadbox. And affordable."

"We need one. I don't want them to trace your call."

"What am I calling about?"

"Tell me what you think of this." She held the notepad at arm's length in the traditional pose of a woman whose eyes are aging faster than she's willing to accept. "Conrad Lawton Littleton of Braddocks Beach, Ohio, did not die of natural causes, and the killer is going to get away with murder unless you open an investigation immediately. He was being treated for heart problems, and his death looked like a heart attack, so the police are not investigating. But he was murdered. You need to contact Chief Bennett and command him to order an autopsy. And you'd better hurry, because Mr. Littleton will be embalmed first thing Monday morning. Your first suspect should be his loving wife of thirty-two years, Malvina Lorraine Spruill Littleton."

"Malvina?"

"From literature. James MacPherson. Eighteenth-century Romantic poet."

And I thought my obscure name, after my mother's favorite mystery magazine, was a burden.

"Well?"

I examined Sam's plan from all angles. The first question I asked myself was, *Is making a false report to the SBI a federal offense?* Second question, *Is driving the car to aid someone in making a false report to the SBI considered aiding and abetting in the commitment of a federal offense?* Third question, *If I change my legal home-of-record to Braddocks Beach while I spend time in the federal penitentiary for the aforementioned crimes, would that count toward my residency requirement to receive Aunt Izzy's bequest?* Fourth question, *How did I let myself get involved in this crazy scheme?* "Why can't you talk to them?"

"Because . . ."

"Because why?"

"They might recognize my voice."

Bessie bumped and rocked, and I realized I'd been staring at Sam and not the road. I eased the steering wheel to the left and settled her back on the straight-and-too-narrow. "Have you made a lot of calls to the SBI?"

"A few."

"Why?" I should teach a continuing education course on Teacher Interrogation 101: Keep Asking *Why?* Until the Perpetrator Tells All.

"Only because Chief Bennett is such a bumbling idiot. Somebody needs to be keeping an eye on him."

"Why you?"

"If not me, who?"

With four little words, Sam turned the tables and stumped me in the process. I didn't know the inner workings of Braddocks Beach well enough to comment, but it did seem odd that Sam felt the need to oversee the chief of police. Why not the mayor? Why not the city council? Why not any of the other twelve thousand residents?

"Follow the signs to I-71 North. Should be a right turn soon."

I guided Bessie around the tight curve of the ramp and onto the highway, merging into the considerable traffic. Billboards advertising everything from Cleveland-area tourist attractions to fast-food aimed at the playland-crowd hinted that modern civilization was only fifty miles away.

"How long does it take to trace a call?" Sam asked.

"How would I know?"

"I don't know. I just hoped you would. I don't think we should take any chances, though. Let's make this short and sweet. Conrad Lawton Littleton of Braddocks Beach was murdered, and the chief of police is treating it as a death from natural causes. Please investigate at your earliest convenience."

"Short enough, but too sweet. This isn't an invitation to an afternoon tea. I'd knock off the last sentence."

Sam nodded and scratched on her notepad, ripped the paper off, and handed the scrap to me. "Are your fingerprints on file in the national database?"

"Why?"

"Because I don't want them to be able to trace our call. So are they?"

I focused on the road.

"Well?" she prompted, as if my hesitation hadn't already given me away.

"Yes." I answered her question without blinking an eye. No use trying to hide my irate e-mails to the commander-in-chief of our armed forces, offering advice on how to better run things in Iraq. I don't get involved in politics as a rule, but I became strongly interested in the issue when one of my students from my first class had been killed by a roadside bomb. At that point, the war hit close to my heart. Homeland Security had traced what I thought were anonymous e-mails to my computer at school. That led to a long talk in a sparse room under one bright lightbulb dangling from the ceiling while being interrogated by a giant of a man with rolled-up shirtsleeves revealing a very scary dragon tattoo. I'd suffered nightmares for days. I wasn't held on any specific charges. They'd scanned my fingerprints to run against the database of convicted felons and suspected terrorists. I guess in this age, when we're waging a global war on terrorism, I should be thankful officials investigate any and all threats. Not that I'd threatened anyone. Well, not that I'd intended to *act* on any of those threats.

"We'll need gloves, then. Do you have any?"

"Nope. I'm a mittens girl from way back."

"That'll work." She opened the glove compartment and out tumbled a rainbow of napkins from every take-out joint within a fifteen-mile radius of my Virginia Beach apartment. "Where are they?" Sam asked after sorting and straightening the napkins.

"In a box in the back of my closet. Where do you expect them to be in the middle of June?"

"No need to get snippy. I was just asking. As Queen Bee, you'll probably want to tuck a pair of white gloves in here, should you ever be invited to a last-minute formal tea at Niora Davidson's house. But we don't have time to go back to get some. Wait, I have an idea. Here. This exit. Quick. You've got plenty of room to get over. Go."

I swerved Bessie to the right, flicking on my turn signal as

I went, but a blaring horn indicated I didn't have as much merging room as Sam had led me to believe. I waved an apology through the opened sunroof and swung Bessie down the ramp.

"Yo quiero Taco Bell?" Sam asked.

"Yo quiero el baño," I said in return, and without waiting for an answer I turned into the parking lot. While I headed off to the señoritas' room, Sam sat in the car. I did leave the windows down.

When I returned, Sam was gone, but she emerged from the Taco Bell a few minutes later with two cups in hand, and dangling from her pinky finger was a pair of those thin plastic gloves the taco assemblers wear when stuffing cheese and lettuce into crispy shells. What a resourceful woman Sam was.

We climbed into the car, secured our drinks in cup holders, fastened our seatbelts, and in no time at all were sipping ice-cold Diet Pepsis through long red straws while heading northeast on I-71, still looking for a pay phone. Farms gave way to suburbia. We exited the highway and cruised the next seven exits, but the few pay phones we did find did not meet Sam's standards. Seemed she preferred one that would allow us relative privacy.

I wanted to abandon the mission. Sam did not. We argued. Sam won on the point that I did not want to have to chase down Connie's murderer ourselves, possibly putting our own lives at risk. Best to leave this up to the professionals.

"Stop!" Sam screamed.

I slammed on the brakes, fearing I was about to run over a child or something.

"Turn around," Sam ordered. "I saw a pay phone."

I looked in my rearview mirror. Sure enough, a pay phone encased in a private glass booth was half a block back. So back we went to a tumbled-down family motel that advertised color TV on its marquee. Bessie's four-wheel drive was instrumental in getting us across the bubbled and crumbled parking lot to the solitary phone booth. I suspected nobody had slept at the Quackenberry Family Motor Lodge since the Kennedy era. It didn't make any sense that the motel could be so decrepit and yet the glass phone booth looked as sturdy as the day it had been erected.

The motel may have had vacancies, but the phone booth was overbooked by a family of rats and six hundred or so members of a spider clan, none of which liked being disturbed when Sam eased the door open. The critters didn't seem to faze Sam. They fazed me. A lot. I'm not a big fan of creepy-crawlies.

Squeals of children burning off travel energy at the McDonald's Playland across the street seemed incongruous with the setting. Then again, everything about this "mission" seemed incongruous with my staid life as a third-grade teacher.

Standing outside the booth, we each donned a glove. The sound of my heart pounding in my ears drowned out the sounds of traffic on the nearby highway.

Sam handed me the phone. I held it to my ear while she reached her arm in, deposited a few coins, and punched the number. From memory, I noted.

Momma rat twitched her whiskers at me from beneath an old take-out drink holder, her beady eyes wary and ominous. I stepped backward until the phone cord yanked me to a halt. A spider crawled up my arm, and I brushed it away. Another spider skittered down my neck, and another crawled up my leg. All were swatted without a milligram of remorse and with a bushel full of repulsion.

"State Bureau of Investigation. Cleveland office. How may I direct your call?"

Hearing those words in a not very customer-friendly voice made my knees knock. My thought process switched over to hold and my breathing became labored as it whistled across the mouthpiece. Sam poked me. In the arm. Hard. I swatted her hand. She poked me again and pointed to the phone.

I mustered up every ounce of courage and tried to speak, only every word of Sam's carefully scripted report was gone like a whisper and a wish. Sam poked me again.

"ConnieLittleton'sdeadbecausesomebodykilledhim."

Sam clicked the cradle before I had the presence of mind to mention Braddocks Beach. But how many men named Connie Littleton could have died in this country in the past few days? Unless they searched for a female Connie. A Constance, not a Conrad.

It was then I realized that in my fear I'd used my right hand to steady the receiver. My ungloved hand. I dropped the phone and raced after Sam, who had a five-second head start on me back to Bessie.

My hands shook like I'd just drunk thirty-two grande Colombia Nariño Supremos, making it virtually impossible to slip the key into Bessie's ignition.

"Hurry up!" Sam urged, bouncing in her seat.

That didn't help the situation.

Nor did seeing the flashing blue lights in my rearview mirror.

Chapter Seventeen

Sam amazed me yet again.

She convinced the fiftysomething highway patrolman with a gun that we were two lost, addlebrained tourists from Virginia (thanks to Bessie's license plates) headed toward Chagrin Falls, and we'd used the pay phone to call her cousin Jenny Sue Evans for directions. We were due there for a good old-fashioned pig pickin' to be held in our honor that afternoon. Her southern drawl, although sounding a bit affected to my ears, was a nice touch. But the way she called him "Honey-chile" while batting those baby greens sealed the deal. He never mentioned a call to the SBI. And neither did we.

"Ya'll come back now, ya hear?" the patrolman called to us as we drove off. If there's one thing I've learned in life, it's that Southern-speak is highly contagious.

My legs shivered like Jell-O as I goosed Bessie back onto the road. I turned north on I-71 as if we were indeed heading toward Jenny Sue's house, just in case the patrolman was watching.

"I need something to eat. You hungry?" I asked.

"No thanks. I'm saving room for the pig pickin' in a few hours." She smiled. Sam must be from the school of thought that if you believed what you said was the truth, then it wasn't a lie.

"I'll save room." I smiled back.

We headed north before doubling back south, just in case the patrolman was watching. As soon as we crossed into the next county, I pulled into an Arby's and loaded up on carbs and fat. We were back on the road in two minutes flat, this time heading south toward Braddocks Beach.

Sam scribbled on her notepad as if she were involved in some sort of writing marathon.

"Whatcha working on?" I asked as I dug in the fast-food bag for any fry that might have fallen out of the cardboard holder.

"We have a lot to do before calling on Lorraine again tonight." Sam tapped her pen against her notepad. "Somebody has to know something about Mizizzy's and Connie's deaths. I just can't believe we haven't figured it out yet. What time is it?"

I looked at the clock on Bessie's dashboard. "Going on three o'clock."

"Good. We'll have time to dash into Big-Mart. There's one at the next exit. According to my calculations, you should be running low on clean underwear."

Sam assumed correctly, although I hadn't hit the point where I'd turned a pair inside out for a second wearing.

"And while you get the things you need, I'll check out their gun selection."

"Huh?" If there was one thing I hated, it was guns. Not guns in general, but people with guns. And having a gun in Sam's hands was the scariest thought I'd ever had in my life. "I think we can skip the gun thing, if it's all the same to you."

"It's not all the same to me. We may need protection."

"From asking questions?" That's all I'd committed myself to, and I was standing my ground on that point.

Sam tapped her pen on her tablet. When I glanced over, her mouth wore a thin line of frustration. "Ellery, sometimes you try my patience. We're still just asking questions. Still on the agenda of talk, look, and listen. No danger there. I'm just window-shopping today, in the event we *do* get to the point we need some firepower on our side. I want to have the information I need to make a decision quickly, that's all."

The combination of nervous sweat and French fry grease made my grip on the steering wheel a bit slick. One at a time, I wiped them along my nylon pants. Sam handed me a napkin. I used it to wipe down the steering wheel and then tossed it in the fast-food bag.

"I'd think you'd want to be prepared too. After all, we're

protecting your name here. And it's your backside we're trying to keep out of jail. Now, are you still with me?" She held
out her fist. I glanced at it, then at her face. She seemed to be
holding in another sigh.

I took a few deep breaths to calm my nerves and contemplate
what Sam had said. I didn't want to go to jail, even though I had
full trust in a legal system that would keep me from being convicted based on lack of evidence, let alone not having the killing gene in me. But keeping the Tinsdale name from being
dragged through the mud was another thing. That photomon-
tage on the wall proved the family name carried a great deal of
responsibility. It was up to me to make sure that name carried
on with the respect it was due. It had been part of the Braddocks
Beach heritage for over a hundred and fifty years. Far be it from
me to pull it down in less than twenty-four hours.

We could keep asking questions. Certainly every Braddocks Beach citizen was doing the same thing, trying to make
sense out of all this. The gun thing had just sent me into panic
mode, that's all. I should probably lay off the caffeine. And get
some sleep.

I tapped her fist.

We shopped, and I stocked up on the basic necessities of
life, like underwear and Cheetos.

Before I allowed Sam back into the car, I checked both of
her bags to make sure she wasn't packing heat. She'd picked
up some DVDs and baseball pants for her stepgrandson, but
no gun.

We drove back to Braddocks Beach in relative silence, with
Sam scratching notes on her pad while I imagined question-
asking scenarios where a gun would be helpful. Maybe I
would feel safer if I had one.

Sam helped me carry my bags in, then went down the front
hall to grab my mail. I was just putting the last of the snack
foods away when I heard a scream.

It was Sam.

And it sounded like someone was choking her.

Chapter Eighteen

Ohmygawd, ohmygawd, ohmygawd, ohmygawd—" Sam's screams got louder and louder and higher pitched.

At least I knew she was still alive.

I searched around the kitchen for a weapon suitable for subduing an attacker of unknown size or mental state. A wire basket filled with polished-brass apples caught my eye. I grabbed one and hit the hallway at full stride. I had my arm cocked as I ran from the kitchen. The second I turned the corner, I fired my weapon.

I wished with all my heart and soul that I could take that shot back.

It happened in slow motion, the way Sam's head lifted from the piece of paper she'd been reading, a moment of horror flashing across her face as her lips formed the word *No*. The brass apple hit her in the temple, snapping her head backward, throwing her off balance. She stumbled one, two, three steps, lost her footing on all the envelopes puddled around her on the wood floor, and crashed in a heap at the foot of Aunt Izzy's graceful staircase.

Now it was me screaming, "Ohmygawd, ohmygawd, ohmygawd, oh," as I knelt over a bleeding Sam.

I did, out of courtesy, accompany Sam in the ambulance. Along with George. The big bear of a man stroked Sam's hand.

I don't remember ever feeling worse about anything in my life.

About fifteen minutes into the ride—the nearest hospital being in the big city of Medina where we'd just been at the Big-Mart—Sam's eyes fluttered open. George brushed the hair from her forehead and leaned his bushy face in close.

"Ellery," I heard her say in that clear, bossy Sam voice.

I moved into her line of vision. "I'm so sorry," I told her, my voice catching in my throat.

"Where's the letter?"

"What letter?"

"The one I was reading when you beaned me."

I thought about it but didn't know. Probably trampled by the emergency medical technicians and police who'd responded to my 911 call.

"Please tell me you have the letter!"

"Stop upsetting the patient." The EMT pushed me out of the way and spoke to Sam in soothing tones.

"Turn the ambulance around right now. We need to go back to the house," Sam ordered.

"Ma'am," the EMT said, "we need you to relax. As soon as a doctor has examined you, you'll be on your way back home." The EMT made some notations on his clipboard.

"I'll relax as soon as Ellery gets that letter, and not until." A note of hysteria crept into Sam's voice.

"Ma'am," the EMT said.

"I don't even know—" I started to say.

"Stop the ambulance!" Sam yelled.

"Honey," George cooed.

"Please relax, ma'am," the EMT urged again.

"Stop the ambulance. Right now. Ellery, get out. Get out of this ambulance and go home. Run as fast as you can back to town. Find that letter."

We all stared at each other in stunned silence.

"If you don't stop this ambulance right now I'm going to rip this monitoring equipment off and stop this ambulance with my own bare hands!" Sam reached her right hand over and grabbed the blood pressure cuff, and there was no doubt in my mind she intended to do just that.

The EMT leaned forward and tapped the glass window that separated the driving area from the passenger area. "Pull over," he called to the driver.

The ambulance swayed as it hit the shoulder and then slowed

to a stop. George scooted toward the back and opened the door, motioning for me to exit. Hopping out gracefully was not an option for someone of my size and physical condition, but I did the best I could under the circumstances.

As I stood on the side of the road, I peered through the open door at Sam lying on the gurney. Her face looked pale. She looked exhausted. "Find that letter!" she yelled before her eyelids fluttered shut.

She didn't honestly expect me to run the ten miles back to Braddocks Beach, did she?

George tossed me a cell phone. "Call Charlie's Cab Service. It's listed in my address book. Tell him who you are and that I said to come get you." He looked very apologetic.

The ambulance door slammed shut and pulled away, lights flashing as if it were a matter of life or death. Poor Sam.

Forget Sam. Poor me.

I made the call. Charlie's Cab would be here in twenty minutes. I hurdled the ditch and settled down on the nearest tree stump to wait. Crickets chirped. Mosquitoes buzzed. Horseflies bit. Cars sped past. Then the rain started. A light drizzle at first, but then the raindrops got bigger and pounded my head harder. I looked around the stretches of cornfields with nary a tree or structure to be seen.

A whimper escaped. I wanted nothing more than to go back to my nice, familiar, uncomplicated, and crowded life in Virginia Beach, where there was always a human around when you needed one.

An hour later, I was dry and cozy in my newly purchased sweatsuit at Aunt Izzy's house. My designer outfit had been ruined by the rain, and I'd conceded one shoe in the tug-of-war against the mud along the side of the road when I'd chased Charlie's Cab down the highway.

My plans for the evening included food and sleep.

I made a quick phone call to Hansel and Gretel's. Veralee assured me she could have a magnificent get-well-soon basket delivered to Sam at the hospital within the hour. I almost choked on my tongue when she told me the final total, hitting three digits without benefit of caviar, but I swallowed my surprise and asked if she could put it on my tab. And so it was done. A girl could get used to this way of doing business.

The post-thunderstorm sun was dipping in the western sky, and I had my Milano-cookie appetizer at the ready. A thick-crust, ham-and-pineapple pizza would be delivered in less than thirty minutes. The only thing that would make me happier at this moment was if I'd found the letter Sam had been reading when I'd knocked her unconscious.

Someone had straightened the house in my absence: rugs back in place, blood mopped from the parquet floor, mail stacked in a nice neat pile and tucked amid the Royal Dalton figurines on the lowboy. But the opened letter and its envelope were nowhere to be found. I'd searched the trash cans in the event my housecleaning fairy had thrown it away but found not a trace of any discarded mail.

How important could a letter be? I mean, Sam had obviously read it and knew its contents.

The phone rang, the old-fashioned clapper-against-metal sound jangling my nerves. I walked over to the black rotary-style telephone sitting on a small table by the front door. It rang again as I laid my hand on the handset, sending vibrations all the way up my arm. It seemed to be warning me of impending danger.

I answered it anyway. "Ellery Tinsdale."

"Do you have the letter?"

"Sam, are you okay?"

"I'm fine. Do you have the letter?"

"I just can't tell you how truly, truly sorry I am—"

"Do you have the letter?"

I twisted my fingers in the cloth-covered cord that had been conveying phone calls since the 1950s. She sounded upset. I didn't want to upset her any more. But I couldn't lie to her. "No," I whispered.

"Where is it?" she whispered back.

I explained how the house had been straightened in my

absence. Silence. I watched gold balls on the anniversary clock spin first one way, then the opposite.

"Hold on," Sam said. I listened while she sent George off in search of a vending machine. "I'm back. Who all was in the house?"

I hadn't paid much attention, to be honest. I'd been more concerned about Sam's condition. Added to the confusion had been Chief Bennett's threats to haul me in on assault charges as soon as he got a statement from Sam. She needed to understand it was an accident. "I'm sorry, Sam. I didn't really mean to hurt you. I thought you were being attacked, the way you were screaming."

I could hear her eyes rolling back in their sockets. "I told you it's okay. Forget about it. We have to find that letter. Who all was in the house?"

I closed my eyes and replayed the scene in my mind. "The two EMT guys, Chief Bennett, the couple from across the street—"

"Doris and Doodles Rogers."

"Yes, them. George, of course. And the pie lady."

"Reba? What was she doing there? She lives on the other side of town."

"Wait. Let me think. She said something about making a condolence call to Lorraine."

"Oh, geez, I forgot about that. It's my guess that Doris straightened the house. You need to go talk to her. Find out what she did with the letter."

"What is so important about a letter?" Sam's dramatics were wearing on me in my tired and hungry state.

"You have to swear on your Aunt Izzy's grave that you won't breathe a word of it to anyone."

"Who would I tell? I don't know anyone but you."

"Swear."

"Okay, I swear." I held up two fingers the way I'd done when I'd taken the Brownie pledge back in first grade.

"The letter was from a DNA testing facility." Sam was whispering again. I pushed the handset to my ear to the point it hurt.

"It provided proof that Conrad Lawton Littleton was the biological sibling of Betty Anne Payne Fitzsimmons."

Sam seemed to be waiting for my shocked gasp, but the information meant nothing to me.

"Cordy is engaged to Betty Anne's son, Robert Fitzsimmons Junior, known to all who love him as Fitz-Two."

"God bless you," I said.

"I didn't sneeze," Sam snarled. "That's his name. F-I-T-Z-T-W-O. As in Fitz the second."

I drew a mental genealogy tree of the Fitzsimmons and the Littletons, what little I knew of them anyway. Something seemed wrong, but I just couldn't figure out what.

"That makes Cordy and Fitz-Two first cousins. It's illegal for first cousins to marry in Ohio."

"Then it's good they found out now before they spawn two-headed babies—"

"I'm sure you understand," Sam interrupted me, "what the emotional consequences would be if that information got into the wrong hands. For Cordy and Fitz-Two. And for Betty Anne."

I sighed and nodded, even though Sam couldn't see me. Was it really anyone else's business but theirs?

"But I don't imagine the social consequences are as obvious to you. Fitzsimmons are relatively new to town, less than five years. Littletons have been here almost as long as the Tinsdales. Cordy and Fitz-Two's children will have Braddock blood running through their veins. That's very, very important to Betty Anne. On the flip side, Fitz-Two is being groomed for governor, with rumblings of a possible presidential run in his future. That's very important to Lorraine, who is a power-by-relation believer of the worst sort."

"I see."

"I don't think you do, El. This kind of information would be kept hush-hush at all costs, or the consequences could be severe."

"You mean like social outcasting or blackmail?"

"No, I mean like murder."

Chapter Nineteen

So much for pizza and a movie. There was sleuthing to be done.

Sam had given me my talk, look, and listen orders. Within ten minutes I was headed out the door to Lorraine's house to offer my condolences. I was to play the role of Queen Bee by being friendly and gracious, and casually asking if anyone had seen anyone lurking around the Littletons' house last night.

Catching a glimpse of myself in the gilded mirror hanging over Aunt Izzy's mahogany lowboy, I drew a modicum of confidence from my outfit. My black crepe tunic-top-and-pants outfit, which I'd found hanging on the back door of the laundry room, courtesy of Chiquita, made me feel like the television character Maude. My fashion consultant had completed the outfit with lots of chic and jingly jewelry. I felt sassy and poised. Except for the brown clogs. I hope nobody reported the fashion faux pas back to Sam, who had told me to wear the new black shoes. I didn't want to upset her with the news that one was stuck in the mud somewhere along State Route 913 South. She'd been through enough today.

Tucking a note for the pizza delivery man to put the pie in the refrigerator (I'd already arranged to put the cost, and a hefty tip, on my account), I headed up Charleston Street.

The Littletons' front screen door had been propped open with a large potted hibiscus plant and the solid-oak front door secured with a metal chair. I stepped across the threshold into the brightly lit, gleaming oak-floored entryway and followed the sounds of voices to the kitchen, where I found a sea of strangers. My fight-or-flight instincts warred again. This time

I chose to fight, as I was on a mission on behalf of Sam, who was lying in a hospital bed on account of me.

"Miss Tinsdale, nice to see you." Henrietta Zucker stepped forward and took from my hands the tray of sliced-up beef sticks and cheddar cheese wheels (dug, at Sam's instruction, from a Hickory Farms basket tucked in the back of the closet under Aunt Izzy's stairs). She set it on the counter, where it stood out like a cheap suit at a meeting of Mafia dons. The Braddocks Beach potluck queens had been busy again. I surveyed a sea of bubbling spinach dips, tempting pound cakes, and mountains of fruit kebabs.

Henrietta pulled me into a group of four other people. Introductions were made. Talk was generic: the tragedy of it all, the shortness of life, et cetera. This wasn't getting me anywhere. The sooner I got the answers Sam wanted, the sooner I could get back home and into my comfy clothes.

"So," I asked, ever so casually. "Lorraine will inherit everything, I gather?"

Judging by the slack-mouthed stares I received, that was a tacky question. No answer was forthcoming. I made my apologies and slipped from the group. This Investigative Queen Bee role was a tough gig.

I followed my nose to the backyard, where a man in a LICENSED TO GRILL apron and matching chef's toque stood over a half-barrel grill. Flames licked at rows of burgers and brats, filling the air with the delicious aroma of sizzling meat. But before I could grab a plate and belly up to the picnic table, I spotted Doris and Doodles. *Work first, eat second,* I could hear Sam say. I walked toward the couple, who were dressed in matching white Oxford shirts and navy blue sweaters tied around their shoulders.

"I appreciate your help this afternoon," I said, dragging a plastic chair behind me along the asphalt.

"How's Sam doing?" Doris asked.

I squeezed myself into the seat, the armrests pressing painfully into my hips. I hoped there was a crowbar handy to get me out. "Fine. The doc is keeping her overnight for observation.

You really helped me out by cleaning up the house. I don't do well with blood."

Doris smiled. "I was a scrub nurse for twenty years. Doesn't faze me. There wasn't much to be cleaned up, anyway."

"I do appreciate it, though. And stacking the mail. I guess that's what Sam slipped on in the first place." She did, technically. No need to mention the apple beaning. "But there was a letter that had been opened that seems to be missing. I checked the trash cans but couldn't find anything."

"Was it important?"

According to Sam, it could be a matter of life and death. But I didn't want to be overly dramatic here. "It contained some information that's important, yes."

"I don't remember seeing an opened letter, do you, Doodlebug?" She turned her questioning gaze to Doodles. He shook his head, his fish-belly-white jowls undulating like a bulldog's.

"Are you sure?" I asked.

"Quite. I'd never throw anything out, anyway." She seemed somewhat offended.

"Did anyone else help you clean up?"

"No. If I remember correctly, everyone went out to watch Sam being loaded into the ambulance."

Sad comment on society in general, I thought.

A woman joined us, and Doris introduced her as Scootch McKenzie, a weekend riding instructor at the Circle BB stables. That explained the slightly inappropriate cowgirl outfit. The name sounded familiar, but I couldn't place the face. Then it hit me. She was the designer-dressed mole-on-the-neck (now covered by a hideous cow-print scarf) lady from last night. What was her connection? Rummage sale coordinator?

Scootch excused herself and Doris, and the two stepped away to hold a hushed conversation. I'm no expert in body language, but this one had *top secret* written all over it. I strained my ears but couldn't hear a single word. When Doodles cleared his voice, I realized he was watching me watching his wife. Another social faux pas, I felt certain.

I turned my attention to Doodles. Something about him

gave me the willies. Dressing like his wife's twin was disconcerting, but there was something more. Maybe his reclusive
demeanor. Maybe the bushy eyebrows poking above the Harry
Potter glasses. Maybe the way he looked at me as if I was
wearing skunk perfume. Maybe it was something as simple as
a grown man allowing himself to be called Doodlebug.

The silence hung between us like a bulging water balloon. I
sipped my drink and crunched the ice. I was in looking-and-
listening mode.

"Doris told me she told you what I overheard."

I about jumped out of my skin at his voice. But here was the
opening I needed. "Something to the effect that you overheard
Lorraine say, 'One of us is going to have to kill him.'"

"Correction. It wasn't Lorraine."

I felt my eyebrows slide up toward my hairline. This was
interesting. I waited, but Doodles' lips were pressed tightly
together in a way that reminded me of a baby refusing a spoon-
ful of creamed spinach.

"Who was it then?" I asked.

His gaze focused on his feet. I glanced down and realized
why I didn't like him. He wore the same Docksider shoes
that husband number three had. Bad memories there. "Come
on, Doodles. Sam and I are trying to help find Aunt Izzy's
killer, and we think what you heard may have some bearing
on things."

Still no answer.

"If you won't tell us, will you tell the police?"

A scream broke out from behind me, and I turned in time to
catch a flash of white fur heading for the food. One flying leap
and Pipsqueak landed on the table, right in the middle of the
mountain of burgers and buns, sending them flying. He gobbled
down three before Henrietta Zucker reached him. The chef
looked crestfallen. The hungry people in line looked crestfallen. I had no doubt I looked crestfallen too. I'd been looking
forward to the meal. A heavy forlorn sigh escaped me without
conscious thought.

A group of women rushed to the table to salvage what food

they could. As the commotion died down, I turned back around to finish my grilling of Doodles. Both he and Doris were gone. My investigation wasn't going at all well. Sam would be calling in less than half an hour, and I had nothing to report. I owed it to her to come up with something.

Before I could extricate myself from my chair to search for Doodles, Max stumbled toward me. He collapsed into the chair Doodles had vacated and let his head loll back until he was looking at the sky. He was still drinking out of what could very well be the same bottle we'd left him with this morning. Or it could be a new one, three-quarters empty.

"Hello, Max," I said quietly, not wanting to startle him.

His head rolled forward and dropped into his hand. He started whimpering. "Connie. Connie. Oh, Connie. My best friend in the whole world. Gone," he wailed. "Gone. Why did you leave me, friend?"

I'd bet a dollar to a doughnut he didn't know I was sitting two feet from him. Even though I didn't feel comfortable listening in on the private conversation he was having with his dead friend, I might get some information to give to Sam. I leaned in closer.

He continued talking to himself. "Why did you do this to Lorraine? Why did you sign everything over to Cordy, leaving your wife of thirty-two years homeless? Penniless. Poor Lorraine. Poor, poor Lorraine." Max's head swayed from side to side. "And you left me to break the news. She'll kill me. Kill me dead. Save me a seat in heaven, buddy, cuz I'll be joining you soon." His head dipped a bit lower, lower, lower, until it was halfway to the driveway, at which point the rest of his body followed suit and he ended up in a rumpled, passed-out heap at my feet.

The topic of how to properly deal with drunken men had never been covered in Madame Rowena's school. After all, we were being taught how to be polite young Southern belles, and shouldn't ever have to concern ourselves with the seedier sides of life. But it just didn't seem dignified for this well-respected barrister to be lying in the driveway. He'd saved me from embarrassment the previous evening by keeping me out of jail. I felt it my duty to return the favor.

I wormed myself loose from the chair, rolled Max to his back, grabbed him by the heels, and dragged him behind the detached garage and out of the glare of the spotlights and curious stares. There wasn't much wiggle room, with the overgrown bushes, mounds of decaying leaves, discarded tree limbs, and rusting lawn furniture piled in the small area between the garage and the faded white picket fence, but I managed to get him settled out of sight. Now to get some hot coffee and cold towels. I paused to catch my breath, straighten my clothes, pick twigs from my hair, and search in the underbrush for my left shoe.

My groping hand came across something hard and cold. Upon further touching, I realized it wasn't my shoe but a T-shaped handle. I wrapped my fingers around it and pulled out an aluminum boat oar. At first, I thought it was covered with mud. On closer inspection, I realized the Hershey-chocolate-looking substance was long-dried blood.

If I didn't miss my guess, the blood belonged to my dearly departed Aunt Izzy.

Chapter Twenty

The inside of the holding cell at the Braddocks Beach police station hadn't changed much in the past twenty-four hours. There was a new stain on the pillow and a greenish yellow slug trail I hadn't noticed before. The odor of mildew was so strong I could taste it. The steady *drip, drip, drip* of the sink recalled to memory a history lesson describing the old Chinese water torture. I was only a few drips away from confessing all my sins.

A cockroach skittered across the faded-gray linoleum. I watched him disappear in the gaping crack where the wall met the floor. The cell was so cold I contemplated wrapping myself up in the scratchy, moth-eaten blanket.

Having dispatched the deputy in charge on a coffee-and-burger-procuring mission, Chief Bennett himself stood at the steel-barred doorway that separated the holding area from the small office. He stared at me, his sole prisoner this Saturday night, with one arm on the bar, worrying a toothpick with the intensity of a kindergartner trying to wiggle out his first front tooth. My skin crawled under his beady-eyed gaze. I crossed my arms, rubbed my biceps, and turned away from him.

I had no hope of rescue. Sam was still in the hospital, no doubt unaware of my predicament. Max, to the best of my knowledge, was sleeping off his bender behind the Littletons' garage. I sighed. I didn't even have any more fake friends to provide me an alibi, let alone spring me from the pokey.

Despite two hours of inquisition, I'd stood firm by my statement that I had never before seen that bloody oar in my life. Chief Bennett refused to believe me. He insisted I was trying to dispose of the murder weapon, since his conclusion about the blood agreed with mine. He'd ordered the young police officer to bag and tag it for delivery to the forensics lab in Cleveland. Of course, my fingerprints would be all over it.

I couldn't get Bennett to see the stupidity of trying to sneak off with something as unwieldy as an oar when the area was crowded with witnesses. The chief reminded me that most criminals are stupid, which is why they are often easy to catch.

So why *had* I stepped from behind the garage holding the oar? A question I'd been asking myself repeatedly. I know why I'd brought it out; I wanted to turn it over to the police. But why had I pulled it from the leaves in the first place? Hard to explain that when my fingers had wrapped around the smooth surface, it was as if some force had taken control of my brain and had messaged my muscles to pull it out and examine it. A cold draft swept across the back of my neck at the memory. I scrubbed it away.

A phone rang, and I looked through the bars. Chief Bennett gave me one last narrow-eyed glare before turning and exiting stage left. I felt some tension flowing from my shoulders as I continued pacing the ten-step-by-ten-step cell.

"Yes, sir. Yes, sir. Yes, sir." Chief Bennett's end of the conversation harmonized with the dripping sink. I teetered one inch closer to insanity.

The sound of a phone slamming into its cradle stopped me midstride.

A few moments of silence, then I heard Chief Bennett's voice again, this time with a hint of desperation. It piqued my interest, so I sidled up to the steel bars and cupped my ear in the direction of the office. His voice rose in agitation, echoing off the cement walls. ". . . SBI sending someone down to claim the body. They'll do the autopsy and launch a full investigation into why the M.E. didn't order one. . . . I'm not panicking. . . . I'm not. I'm not. I'm just not going down with you. I'm doubling the payoff. In my account by ten. I've got a flight booked to Mexico in twelve hours—"

He was interrupted by another person in the outer room.

"I'm gonna have your butt on a platter, Bennett." I never thought I could be so happy to hear Sam's harpy voice.

I heard the phone slam back into its cradle.

"We don't take kindly to false imprisonment," Sam said, her voice bordering on shrill. "Especially of one of our most esteemed citizens. Here's the bail money." The sound of a soft thud filtered through to my ears. "Judge Hildebrand said I could give it to you, and you can turn it over tomorrow morning. Now give me the keys so I can let Ellery out."

I heard a jangling, and a moment later Sam appeared at the gated doorway. Sporting green surgical scrubs and a white bandage wrapped around her head like a crown, she looked tired and pale. But fluorescent lights make everyone look that way, don't they? Guilt for being responsible for her weakened condition stabbed my gut. A glimpse of fire shooting from those green eyes assured me that Feisty Sam was alive and well.

She had me sprung in two shakes of a spaniel's tail.

I wrapped my arms around my savior, smushing her face to my bosom. "I have never been so happy to see anyone in my life!"

"Come on," she mumbled after extricating herself from my death grip. "No time for sentimental claptrap now. We have work to do."

Leaving Chief Bennett with a one-fingered salute (okay, not a proud Queen Bee moment, but fatigue and hunger had me feeling very churlish), we exited the building.

"Are you feeling better?" I asked after I'd replaced the stale jail air in my lungs with fresh night air.

"Got a headache. Doctor says it could last a few days. He gave me something for the pain. Said I shouldn't operate heavy machinery. Or drive." She opened the driver's side door of a station wagon and slid behind the wheel.

I hesitated a moment before opening the door on the passenger side and folding myself into the tiny space. I waited, my chin resting on my knees, but she didn't put the key in the ignition. Phew. Instead, she reclined her seat a bit, pressed her hands to her eyes, and started talking.

"Doris called me at the hospital and told me you found Aunt Izzy's murder weapon."

"Maybe. A boat oar." I gave her the condensed version of what had happened. She kept asking questions until she'd wrested every last detail from me, including the part about how I'd come to be behind the garage in the first place. Chief Bennett could learn a few things from her. "Oh, and guess what a drunken Max told me? Well, I don't think he was aware of my existence. He was talking to himself, but I listened."

"What?"

Sam sounded as weary as I felt, so I got straight to the point. "Connie had signed everything over to Cordy, leaving Lorraine destitute. No money. No home."

Sam sighed and ran her fingers along her head bandage.

"Why would he do that?" I asked.

"I don't know, but if Lorraine found out, she might have killed him." Sam shook her head and then grabbed it with both hands. She drew a sharp intake of breath, held it, then spoke again. "If the way Connie manipulated his assets to leave Lorraine destitute was the secret project he and Mizizzy were working on, then Lorraine may have killed Mizizzy for whatever role she had. But why kill Connie if she would lose everything upon his death? At least with him alive, she still had a roof over her head and a position in society. It doesn't make any sense."

The windshield was starting to steam up. Sam inserted the key in the ignition, switched it to the accessories position, and powered down the windows. The fresh breeze across my cheeks served like a gentle slap and cleared the cobwebs from my sleepy mind.

We sat in silence. My thoughts went existential while Sam fell asleep. I listened to her steady breathing and gave into the bone-weary fatigue infusing itself throughout my body. Hunkering down in the seat, I tried to make myself as comfortable as possible. Making the mile walk to Aunt Izzy's house held about as much appeal as climbing Mount Everest.

My eyes drifted shut, then opened a moment later when I heard a car door slam. It took every ounce of energy I could muster to turn my head a fraction of an inch to see where the noise had come from. An engine started. Brake and backup lights illuminated behind us. Tires squealed as a white pick-up truck zoomed out of its parking spot and rocketed out of the area.

In the diffused light from the illuminated BRADDOCKS BEACH POLICE STATION IST PRECINCT sign, I saw the scowling face of the driver. Chief Bennett, whom I'd just overheard blackmailing someone on the phone. Then I remembered his plans to skip the country. I should have told Sam this first. Blame my lack of cognitive function on fatigue. The synapses were firing very slowly and eventually arrived at a course of action.

"Follow that car!" I yelled to Sam.

Chapter Twenty-one

Sam sat up, shook her head, and turned her key in the ignition, and we were laying rubber out of the parking lot in hot pursuit. We hit the road. Literally. So hard my jaw snapped shut. I bit my tongue, and my mouth filled with the coppery taste of blood.

Too late did I remember Sam's doctor's order not to drive. I fumbled with my seatbelt, locking myself in for what promised to be a very bumpy ride.

Sam drove the wagon like it was the Batmobile and she was the caped crusader pursuing the Joker. But when we hit Tinsdale Circle, there wasn't a pair of taillights to be seen.

Sam took the turn onto Lexington on two wheels. The glow from the gaslight-style street lamps in the tourist district blurred together like a time-lapse photo as we raced through the deserted town. I braced my right hand against the dashboard and grabbed the "hang on, honey" handle above my head with my left hand, enabling me to rest my chin on my bicep to keep my teeth from knocking together whenever we hit a bump, which was about every two seconds.

Sam hung a right at the Strange Bedfellows Book Store and headed east on Braddocks Beach Boulevard. I diagnosed myself with side-to-side whiplash as the car rocked and settled itself back on all four tires.

"Why are we following Chief Bennett?" Sam raised her voice above the roar of the air blowing in the opened windows.

"We aren't technically following anyone, are we?" I scanned the streets again, but still no sign of Chief Bennett's—or anyone else's—vehicle.

"I saw him turn as if he were heading for home. I'm taking a different route, and with any luck, we can be there ahead of him. Now tell me what you've got on him." Sam licked her lips.

I did, too, but only because my mouth was so dry. When was the last time I'd had anything to eat or drink? Hours ago. Visions of Sugar Smacks danced in my head. That and Cap'n Crunch were my breakfasts of choice. A carryover from childhood.

"Ellery, did you hear me?"

Enough food fantasies. I needed to focus. "Because he's expecting a payment from someone he's blackmailing, and then he's skipping the country to Mexico. At high noon."

The force of one g pushed me back against the seat as the wagon accelerated under Sam's heavy-footed influence. I didn't dare glance at the speedometer. I'd just rather not know some things.

The community grid quickly gave way to a narrow two-lane road bordered on both sides by deep ditches and untamed wilderness. No-man's-land. I felt a frisson of apprehension trickle down my spine.

"I knew that guy was as crooked as Lombard Street!" She postured herself over the wheel like Cruella de Vil in *101 Dalmatians*, concentrating on the dark road ahead. "We need to get him before he skips town. Nothing will give me more satisfaction than seeing his fat butt behind bars. See how he likes it!"

Sam was starting to scare me.

What do I mean starting to? She'd been scaring me since the first time we'd met.

"Doris, who's been working for us by the way, said Scootch pulled her aside at the Littletons' to tell her that one hundred thousand dollars had been wired into Chief Bennett's bank account late yesterday. She traced it to a Swiss account, but the beauty of those accounts is their anonymity."

"How in the world can someone who teaches riding lessons have knowledge of high-finance transactions?"

Sam laughed. "Scootch is the manager of the BBB&T branch on the circle. Today, well, yesterday now, she'd run the rodeo for physically and mentally handicapped kids. It's an annual event. She'll be back in her Oleg Cassini pinstripe suit come Monday morning."

"Black and white horizontals more like, for breaching the Banking Privacy Act."

"Nobody needs to know about that, okay?" Sam yanked the wheel to the left and we swerved off the country road onto a dirt path. We bounced along at a speed way too fast for the conditions. I heard the bottom of the car scrape the ground occasionally, but Sam plowed on.

I tightened my grip on the handle and held it so tight I lost the feeling in my hands. "Has it occurred to you that this might be a job for the police?"

"Chief Bennett is the police. Ya think he's going to arrest himself?"

"Good point. But what are we doing?"

"I'm working out a plan." Sam slammed on the breaks and my head rocked forward, banging against the dashboard. When I looked up, the bumper of the car was kissing the trunk of a huge tree. "We're gonna have to hoof it from here." Sam was out of the car like a shot, using the tiny beam of her keychain flashlight to light her way.

Not having the benefit of any light whatsoever, since the sliver of a crescent moon was hiding behind the clouds, I scrambled after her. Thank goodness for the white bandage around her head. It served as a weak homing beacon.

Sam's surgical scrubs and Nikes were more suitable for subversive nighttime field ops. I slogged along in my open-backed clogs and feared yet another new outfit would be ruined after this woodsy trek.

Sam stopped short at the edge of a clearing. I pulled up next to her and bent over, trying to gulp some oxygen into my lungs so they would stop screaming at me.

"Good. We beat him. We have the element of surprise on our side. How are your karate skills?"

"Nonexistent."

"Any hand-to-hand combat experience?"

"Nope."

"Any chance you're carrying?"

"Carrying what?"

"A piece."

"A piece of what?"

"A gun. A taser. Pepper spray. Any sort of weapon."

"Do you watch a lot of police shows on TV or something?"

"George does. I sit with him, knit, and half pay attention. I wish I at least had my size-fifty needles with me right now."

"So we're without weapons?" I swallowed back the rock of fear lodged in my throat.

"No. We have you."

"Me?" I pulled myself up to a standing position.

"You knocked him down twice, remember? When you first came to town and at the beach. You can do it again. If you crouch behind that trash can there." She pointed at a small shadow on the left corner of a building that looked like some sort of hunting cabin. "I'll be on the other side and provide a distraction. You knock him down, and I'll rush over and grab his gun."

A gun? I didn't like the sounds of this. *Someone could get hurt. And that someone could be me.*

"I think I hear a car. Hurry and get into position." Sam disappeared across the clearing.

I really didn't like Sam's plan at all, but I didn't have a better one.

I scurried behind the designated can, pinching my nose shut against the aroma of a compost heap. The sound of an engine, the crunching of tires on rocks, then a triangle of light sweeping across the lot indicated Chief Bennett's arrival. I was thankful for my black outfit, for no matter how hard I tried, I couldn't fit my entire big body behind the three-foot-tall-by-two-foot-wide tin trash can.

A cramp pinched my calf, but I dared not move. As always happened when playing hide-and-seek as a kid, my kidneys kicked into overdrive. I Kegeled the seconds away.

My sense of hearing was on heightened alert in the darkness.

Car engine off. Door opening. Feet on ground. Door shut. Silence.

No sound of him walking. Was he just standing there? What was he doing?

I peeked around and saw the chief. Still in uniform. Complete with gun belt.

And he was looking straight at me.

His hand went to his hip. Very slowly, he flipped the flap covering his gun and slid it out of his holster. He lifted it and pointed it right in my direction.

"Don't shoot!" I yelled, raising my hands and rising from my hiding place.

Chief Bennett jumped, but held onto the gun. "What the hell is going on?"

"We've got you surrounded," Sam called from somewhere in the darkness on the other side of the driveway. "Drop your gun or I'll shoot."

Chief Bennett swung about and fired in the direction of Sam's voice. Sam yipped.

"Come out and show your gun." Chief Bennett called Sam's bluff.

I took two steps forward to rush him, but froze when he turned and pointed the gun back in my direction. I only saw it because my movement must have set off a motion detector and lights flooded the entire front of the cabin.

He used his gun to motion for Sam and me to line up in front of his car. Sam didn't appear to have been hit by the bullet, but her skin tone resembled that of a fish's underbelly.

"I thought you were a goddamned raccoon behind there. I should have shot you. An honest mistake. But now I need to make it look like an accident."

Silence. Well, more like lack of talking. The sound of my beating heart was deafening.

"Okay, inside. And don't try any funny stuff."

I couldn't think clearly enough to try any funny stuff. My thought process had shut down to the point where I had a difficult time just trying to walk.

"Hands over your head, where I can see them."

I raised mine higher to make sure they were visible to the man with the gun. I hoped Sam followed the order. I couldn't see her because she was behind me, but if she didn't follow orders, she'd take a bullet. But knowing how Sam prepares for every eventuality, she probably had a bulletproof vest on under her scrubs. There was nothing between that slug and my heart but a few layers of fat.

I picked my way along a pebbled path that meandered from the driveway to the steps of a small porch. The lower step groaned under my weight, and it groaned again when I stepped off it.

"It's unlocked," Chief Bennett grunted when I stopped at the front door.

I turned the knob and the door swung open to darkness. I walked as far as the light from outside spread. Sam bumped up against my back. I could feel her shaking. I sort of felt sorry for her. But then again, it was entirely her fault that we were even in this predicament. I no longer counted the number of times I'd waxed poetic about my simple, uncomplicated life back in Virginia Beach.

An overhead light flared on, illuminating a sparse, one-room cabin. The smell of day-old tuna casserole permeated the air. My stomach heaved at the scent. Or the fear. I wasn't sure which.

Chief Bennett pulled two rickety wood chairs back to back, then motioned for us to take a seat. He soon had us trussed up like two Thanksgiving turkeys. Amazing he could do it with one hand while holding the gun steady in the other. I wondered if this was a special skill they taught at the police academy.

With one last yank against the bonds holding my wrists in a painful angle against the chair's legs, he rose from the floor and headed for a closet I'd overlooked. He mumbled to himself, obviously not at all happy with the turn of events.

"So who were you blackmailing?" Sam's voice sounded strong and clear.

Sam's question went unanswered while the chief continued throwing personal items into a black Gold's Gym bag.

"I've figured it all out. A hundred grand in your account yesterday and the phone call Ellery overheard tonight. You're blackmailing someone and heading for Mexico."

Chief Bennett paused and stared at Sam as if the information she'd just shared with him was not computing. The muscles in his jaw tensed, then relaxed. "You're not exactly in a position to be asking questions, Ms. Greene." He spat out the name as if it were a wad of chewing tobacco. "But now that I think about it, you might be worth more to me alive than dead, after all."

I would have hugged him at this bit of news, if I weren't still tied to the chair.

"If I tell you who I've been blackmailing, you can use it either to do the blackmailing yourself, or you can nail the murdering bastard's balls to the wall, which is all I've been wanting for the past twenty-five years, except it's been such a lucrative source of income."

I'd thought I was maxed out in nervousness, but when Chief Bennett began tapping his gun against his lip and pacing in small, increasingly tighter circles around us, I thought my nerves would pop from my skin like springy snakes from a jokester's can of peanuts. I tucked my feet as tight under my chair as possible, for fear he'd trip over my foot and fall and the gun would discharge and shoot me through the heart. I doubted Sam would be as cautious. In fact, she might trip him on purpose. The steam valve on my nerves released, and I emitted a loud "Eek."

"What the hell's wrong?" Bennett stopped and waggled his gun in my direction.

"Nothing," Sam answered for me. This was good, because I seemed incapable of answering for myself.

"Okay, how's this for a plan?" He began pacing and tapping again. "I tell you the big secret, then leave you here and hope that somebody comes to check out the cabin before you die of starvation."

I heard Sam's sharp intake of breath. My stomach groaned at the thought. Chief Bennett must not realize it was only a matter of hours before I reached that point. I'd almost rather have the bullet and get it over with quickly. Almost—

"Either way, I'll be safely out of the country." He stopped his pacing right in front of Sam, whose back was to mine. Even though I craned my neck, I couldn't see his face, but the emotionless way he spoke sent a pins-and-needles feeling up my spine and down my arms.

"So here's the story. Thirty years ago, this punk kid showed up on my South Side Chicago beat. Small-town boy blinded by the lights of the big city."

Chief Bennett began pacing again, this time in slow, goose-stepping circles around us. I caught a glimpse of his face as he rounded in front of me. The best way to describe it was crazed and maniacally haunting.

"His parents must have had rocks for brains. They thought he was at college, but somehow he had the tuition funneled to his personal account. Set himself up a life of sex, drugs, and rock 'n' roll. Living the dream."

The chief continued in a monotone of the chilling kind. "The party guy fell in love with a flashy, long-legged Jezebel and paid her well for her exclusive services for three weeks, until he ran out of money. Then she tried to leave, and he killed her. A butcher knife right through her heart.

"I was a young cop on patrol, and I caught him dumping the body. He promised me a lot of money to help him and to keep me quiet. He's been paying steadily ever since. A thousand dollars a month, all tucked away in a bank account. And now the guilt's wearing on him. He's not as careful as he used to be. It's only a matter of time before he goes down. I'm not going with him." Chief Bennett stopped talking but continued circling. His footsteps shuffled against the bare wood floor. The steady scratchy steps were much worse on the psyche than the dripping faucet. The Chinese could learn a thing or two about torture from the chief.

Bile rose in the back of my throat. *So this is what fear tastes like.*

The footsteps stopped in front of Sam. I turned every which way, but I couldn't see Bennett's face. I could hear his words, spoken in a low, emotionless tone. "That young man to which I refer, Ms. Greene, is none other than your esteemed Mayor Twiddy."

"No!" Sam shouted. I felt her chair move as if she were trying to get out of it. "I don't believe you. You're lying!"

"That's the truth, as ugly as it may be."

"It's a lie. I know that Mayor Twiddy graduated from Miami University. He didn't miss a semester. His parents went down to visit him once a month. You're a big fat liar, Bennett."

"Believe what you want, but you can make a fortune off that information. Trust me."

I'd watched enough cop shows with my father many years ago to recognize the sound of a Glock being cocked. "I believe you," I piped up. "I never liked the guy from the first time I met him."

"That's what I want to hear. You're a much wiser woman than you look, Miss Tinsdale."

I heard another click. Silence. As if I'd suddenly gone deaf. I closed my eyes and felt my heart pounding a loud and steady rhythm. I was still alive. For a second there I thought I'd died and just didn't know it yet.

"I'll leave you two here to contemplate what you'll do with the information I've just given you." Chief Bennett was on the move again, this time heading for the closet. He lifted the unzipped bag over his shoulder and headed for the front door.

"Here's something else to think about if you get out of here alive. Ask Mayor Twiddy about a certain Viagra pill slipped into Connie's chicken salad on Friday night. In Connie's case, it was deadly. That might be worth another grand per month for you."

Sam inhaled sharply, and I felt her chair vibrating. "You lying piece of crap! Mayor Twiddy would never have killed Connie. They were friends. They worked together to make Braddocks

Beach what it is. He had no motive. I think you're pointing the finger at Mayor Twiddy when it's you! You're the one who's killed two people!"

The legs of Sam's chair started thumping against the ground as if she and the chair were hopping toward Chief Bennett.

Chief Bennett paused with his hand on the doorknob and pointed his gun. "Settle down now. I don't want you to hurt yourself." His mocking laugh sent shivers down my arms and tremors to my legs. "Trust me, Mayor Twiddy had a motive. One you probably wouldn't believe if I told you, so I'll save my breath. You know what? I almost pity the poor bastard having you two bumbling detectives on his case. Almost worth sticking around to see him suffer." He smiled. One of those smiles you just want to smack off a person's cocky face.

A thought occurred to me. He might know something about Aunt Izzy. "Who killed my aunt?"

"That's for me to know and you to find out."

With that, he saluted us with his pistol, spun on his heel, and disappeared into the darkness.

Sam and I sat, still as stones, and listened to the sound of his car as it heeled around and spun away.

We sat for a few minutes after that, listening to the crickets chirping.

"So now what?" I asked with the last ounce of energy I could muster. Having your life threatened is an emotionally exhausting experience.

"Where's your cell phone?"

"In my truck." I am not a big phone talker, but I carried one around in the event I ever got into an accident and needed to call for help. That was in the days before I tracked down killers in my spare time. I might need to change my ways and start carrying it on my person. "Where's yours?"

"In the pocket of my pants I left back at the hospital."

"A lot of good that's going to do us here."

"Don't worry. I think I have a plan."

If I hadn't been tied to a chair, I would have run as far and as fast away from Sam's "plan" as possible.

Chapter Twenty-two

I let Sam noodle her plan while I thought about my impending death. They said drowning was peaceful, but starvation was slow and painful. The raw, gnawing hunger in the pit of my stomach already ached. Then it hit me—no need to worry about starvation. I would die of dehydration first.

"Help! Help!" My loud, panicked pleas bounced off the raw pine walls. I screamed louder so I couldn't hear the desperation in my own voice.

"Will you please hush up?" Sam shouted when I stopped for a breath. "You're making my head hurt."

"Don't you want to be rescued?"

"Who's going to hear us? It's the middle of the night, so I doubt any hunters or hikers will be wandering by for another four hours or so, and the closest human beings to this cabin are Walt and Gabby Ashford, and they're over a mile away and deaf as doornails anyway, so save your breath."

I screamed again because, one, it felt good to let out my frustration, and two, I didn't have a better idea. I kept screaming until my head felt like seven gnomes were pounding on the inside of my skull with pickaxes.

It wasn't until I stopped screaming that I acknowledged the pain radiating from between my shoulder blades to my extremities. The way Chief Bennett had secured our hands under the lip of the chair seat and tied to a leg (not behind our backs, the way I've seen done in movies) had me bent in an unnatural position. It wasn't all pain. Numbness had thankfully settled into my hands and as a result had rendered them useless in trying to untie the knots.

Sam didn't seem to be having much luck, either. She'd worked herself up to post-marathon panting, and then I heard a crash. I looked over my shoulder and saw Sam, still tied to her chair, lying at my feet. She looked like a turtle on its back. And just as helpless. I felt the giggles start at the top of my diaphragm, and I couldn't stop them. Giggles, sniggers, chortles, working themselves up to uncontrollable guffaws. More panic-driven than circumstance-provoked.

"Queen Bees do not laugh at another's misfortunes."

Her statement, accompanied by her expression of being insulted, only made me laugh harder. Being held hostage was way beyond a misfortune in my book.

Sam lay there staring at the ceiling until I got myself under control. Then, through gritted teeth, she suggested I hop on over and see if I could find a sharp knife in the sink.

Now why hadn't I thought of that?

Hopping with your ankles, knees, thighs, waist, shoulders, arms, and hands tied to a chair is no easy feat. I felt like a snail whose hindquarters had been nailed to the floor—no matter how hard I willed myself in any particular direction, I didn't seem to get anywhere.

Sam watched in silence for a while and then broke into whistles, in an eerie sort of tuneless melody, the likes of which are reserved for harvest-moon nights with the wind howling through the trees while you're sneaking through a graveyard. For the record, I'd done that only once. When I was twelve. Scared me so much I never set foot in a graveyard again, not even during daylight. "Stop, already," I snapped at Sam. "You're driving me nuts."

"I whistle when I'm nervous."

"That's not whistling. That's fingernails on a chalkboard."

Sam stopped. For three heartbeats. Then she started again.

"Stop. Or I. Will. Kill. You."

Despite the fact we both knew my threats were idle, she shut up again. This time for a whole thirty seconds.

When the whistling started again, louder and more eerie than ever, I started cussing. Not just under-my-breath fussing, but loud, anger-releasing epithets that would make a gansta rapper blush. Between that and my grunts and my chair scraping against the wood floor as I dragged it and myself toward the sink, the cacophony reverberating off the wood walls made my head feel like it was hooked up to a bicycle pump and someone kept forcing more and more air into me.

After what seemed like a three-day journey, I parallel parked myself next to the kitchen sink and peered hopefully over my right shoulder into a cracked, stained, and used-to-be-white-but-was-now-a-sickly-yellow porcelain sink. All I saw was a spoon caked with dried cheese sauce. No knife. No sharp object of any kind.

I lost it. A complete, utter, stark-raving-mad hissy fit. I screamed. I shouted. I twisted against the ropes and rocked myself from side to side in a chair whose creaks mocked my every effort.

Then I tipped a little too far to the left and crashed to the floor. I laid there, crunchy crumbs poking into my cheek and spindly chair parts pressing into my spine, and cussed Chief Bennett and Sam and everything that had to do with Braddocks Beach.

The pain in my left shoulder registered on my psyche, so I tried to ease body and chair backward. Lo and behold, I could move my left hand. I could more than move it: I could hold it above my head and wave to Sam! She stared at me for the longest time before celebrating as best she could from her turtle predicament.

The chair's leg had broken off when I'd tipped over, allowing my hand to slip over the top of the spindle. But the other arm and leg still held me prisoner. In the movies, it would have been only a matter of minutes before I worked myself free, but Chief Bennett tied a mean knot that seemed to have been tightened by my struggles.

Sam had the patience of a saint, even though I suspect she was thinking the same thing I was: with each passing second, Chief Bennett was one mile farther away from Braddocks Beach.

Finally, I was free of my bonds. I limited my celebration to an NFL-style end-zone dance before I turned my attention to freeing Sam. Again, snail speed seemed to be the pace of the day.

Even though my body felt as if had just endured a five-day ordeal, it was still dark out when we burst out of the cabin and into the freshness of a pre-dawn wilderness.

Sam took off, jackrabbit that she is, and had the car running by the time I crawled into the passenger seat. She executed a three-point turn that not only was bumpy but also cost us a muffler. Once the nose of the car was pointed in the right direction, we roared off toward town. Sam didn't lift her foot off the gas pedal, let alone apply a modicum of brakes, until we reached the police station.

Sam was already ordering a young police officer around by the time I joined her in the reception area. "Put out an APB. Stop all flights from Cleveland and Dayton and Columbus and Pittsburgh. He's heading for Mexico, and once he's out of the country we'll never catch him!"

The police officer stared from behind the bulletproof Plexiglas. He glanced in my direction and raised his eyebrows as if asking, "Has Mrs. Greene lost her marbles?"

"You don't get it, do you?" Sam's bandage was coming loose around her temple, adding to her crazed look. "He's killed two people, tried to kill us, and I have no doubt he will try to kill again. It's your job to protect society from criminals like him!" Sam's voice, nearly the frequency of a dog's whistle, echoed in the room.

"Chief Bennett?"

"Yes, Chief Albert C. Bennett!"

I thought Sam was going to reach her arm through the saucer-sized opening designed to enable people on the two sides of the glass to speak. The officer must have thought so, too, because he pushed himself sideways to a safe distance before calling over his shoulder for backup.

Over weak coffee and a pack of peanut butter and cheese crackers, we made an official statement to Officer Dave Comp-

ton regarding our hostage situation. He refused to rely on hear-
say that Connie had been murdered. He concurred with Sam's
assessment there was no way Mayor Twiddy, who was scheduled
to read the liturgy at the church this morning, could have murdered anyone. I guess they knew the guy better than I did, but
it still irritated me that these accusations were not taken more
seriously.

We left, assured that the Braddocks Beach police would do
everything in their power to bring Chief Bennett in to face
charges of hostage taking. Attempted murder would be hard
to make stick, considering we had escaped in less than three
hours.

"We could split up and each take an airport," Sam suggested
as we walked across the parking lot. A periwinkle-blue dawn
heralded a new day, reminding me I still hadn't gotten one full
night's sleep since arriving in Braddocks Beach.

"I think we should leave things to the police. Besides, if I
ever lay eyes on Chief Bennett again, I'm likely to kill him myself. Then I'd be in jail. For life. With no possibility of parole."
The few hours I'd spent there had taught me life behind bars is
no life at all.

"I guess." Sam sighed. "And we have plenty of work still to
do around here."

"We do?" My voice cracked.

"Yes. We still don't know who killed Mizizzy. That was our
original goal, remember?"

I wished she hadn't reminded me. I felt a sense of calm thinking our Nancy Drew–scapades were over. But she was right.
Chief Bennett had left this one question unanswered. "What
kind of work do you mean?"

"Same as before. Talk, look, and listen."

"No chasing suspected blackmailers to their remote cabins
in the middle of the night?"

"Far be it from me to point out I did so at your instruction."

Oh, yeah. That had been my idea. Hmmm. I guess I'd gotten a little carried away. I'd learn my lesson, though—leave
the suspect-chasing to the professionals.

We reached the station wagon, and Sam ran her finger along a silver scratch that went the entire length of the car's metallic gold finish. "How am I going to explain this to Reba?"

"This isn't your car?"

"No. It's Reba's pride and joy. She came to visit me at the hospital last night." Sam raised her hand and checked on her head bandage, which had unraveled to the point that she resembled a mummy in a Scooby-Doo cartoon. "Since both George and I rode in the ambulance, we didn't have a way to get home. So, after Reba's visit, she rode back to town with Veralee, who'd also come to visit—thanks for the basket, by the way—and left us her car. Hungry?"

I nodded my head. Those crackers had just whetted my appetite.

"Let's walk on down to Reba's, then. She makes the best cinnamon rolls on earth."

"I love a good cinnamon roll." I do. But then again, I love just about any warm, sweet, gooey confection.

We strolled along the sidewalks at a pace way below Sam's usual skitter. And without running commentary. It was kind of nice, this companionable silence. I peeked out of the corner of my eye and looked beyond the unraveling head bandage. Sam's complexion was a charcoal gray, making the laugh lines look more like worry lines. Her shoulders dropped. Her head listed to the left. No impish sparkle in her eyes. This woman walking next to me was only a shadow of the person I'd met on Friday.

Gauging by the bone-weary fatigue in my own body, I suspected I looked worse for wear myself.

As we stepped onto the northwest arc of the town circle, the aroma of fresh-from-the-oven breakfast treats revived me considerably. I listened to the Westminster chimes coming from a church behind us, followed by six solemn *bong*s. It would be a picture-perfect morning, were we not still feeling the aftereffects of our hostage experience.

Sam knocked on the door of the café, and a young pink-uniformed girl came running to let us in. According to the posted hours, they weren't due to open for another thirty minutes. I didn't think I could wait that long and was fully prepared to force my way inside and beg for a morsel of food and a thimbleful of coffee. I had played Oliver in the summer drama camp production. *Please, sir, may I have some more?*

Sam's connections got us early access. Within minutes, we were settled in the same back booth as yesterday. Without the clatter and chatter of the lunch-hour crowd, the restaurant seemed too pink, the theme too campy, the music too loud. Elvis crooned a song from his Christian years. His deep tenor sang out, "There'll be peace in the valley—" This was as close to a religious service as I'd been in years. I let the spirit move me. Or maybe it was the aroma of cinnamon buns. Either way, I was feeling remarkably better.

Reba brought our coffee. "Morning, ladies. I'm surprised to see you out of the hospital so early this morning, Sam. Since when are doctors available to sign discharge papers before their round of golf?"

Sam laughed. "I wasn't a prisoner. I could release myself anytime I wanted, which I did. Ellery, here, needed me. Oh, and thanks for letting me use your car. You won't believe the adventure we had." Sam told our tale, embellishing it to give Reba's car a starring role and making it sound like the scratch along its side should be treated like a Purple Heart medal. Reba nearly busted the buttons on her pink uniform, she was so proud. Sam laid a hand on Reba's forearm and finished with "And I'll get it back to you just as soon as I get that muffler repaired."

"Thank you so much." Reba clapped her hands in short bursts. "I can't wait to tell the story around today."

"Oh." Sam tick-tocked her finger in warning. "You can't go telling it. Not just yet. Not until Chief Bennett is safely behind bars and has confessed. And remember, Mizizzy's killer is still at large. Give us a few hours. With Ellery and me on the case, we'll have it wrapped up by suppertime."

"If Doodles Rogers doesn't solve it first," Reba said.

"What?" Sam and I said in unison.

"Doodles has been asking around about things. Asked me not to say anything, didn't want to blow his cover."

"What did he ask?" Sam asked, the fire back in her eyes.

Reba seemed to hesitate before pulling up a chair and settling in. It didn't appear that she would be taking our order anytime soon, so I looked around in hopes of seeing the young waitress who had opened the door. I intended to signal her to bring us a mountain of biscuits and jelly. No luck. She was busy wrapping silverware in paper napkins while listening to her iPod.

"He asked a lot about Connie and Lorraine's marriage," Reba said in hushed tones, even though there wasn't anyone around to overhear the conversation. "And if there were any rumors of infidelity and if anyone knew how she got the car—"

"And what did you tell him?"

"That Connie took a lot of meals here, which led me to believe either he liked the food here better or Lorraine wasn't around to cook or eat with him."

"Really?" Sam fell back against her seat and seemed to be digesting the juicy tidbit of gossip. "I swear. Neighbors my whole life, and you'd think I'd know them. So, any rumors of an *affaire de coeur?*"

Reba shook her head. "If so, they were too sneaky for the Mrs. Kravitzes of this town. Hadn't heard of so much as a flirtatious glance."

"And about the new sports car?"

"Cordy told me her mom rented it for the weekend."

"Why?"

"Said it was the kick she needed to pump up her new bad-girl image."

"Why would she tell Zanna she'd won it in a contest?" I asked.

"To make Zanna jealous, maybe?" Reba answered. "It's Zanna's dream car, not Lorraine's."

I shrugged my shoulders and looked at Sam. She didn't answer. Didn't even seem to have heard the question. I could tell by the look in her eyes that the wheels in her head were turning at Mach speed again. This didn't bode well for an early-morning nap.

"What can I get you two ladies to eat?" Reba asked.

"Nothing, thanks. We need to run. Places to go. Things to do. Killers to catch."

"Wait," I called to Sam's back. "I thought we were only going to ask questions."

"We are. Of the killer."

What did Sam know that I didn't want to know?

I followed her anyway, despite my inner voice repeating to me, *Curiosity killed the sleuth.*

Chapter Twenty-three

"How do I look?" Sam asked.

How was I supposed to answer that question? She looked like something that a hyena dragged in now that she had unwrapped the bandage from around her head. Her hair stuck out in every direction, and the bluish-greenish-purplish-yellowish bruise that marked the spot where the brass apple had struck her temple made my stomach squeamish when I looked at it. "Your hair's a bit mussed," I offered with the intention of being truthful.

She combed it with her fingers. "Better?" she asked.

"Yes." It was. But far from not-a-curl-out-of-place Sam standards. "Where are we going now?"

"It's time to talk to Max."

"Do you think he's up yet?"

"Not if he was as drunk as you said last night, but I'm hoping to work that to our advantage. We might get more out of him if he's still under the influence. He's a tough nut to crack when he's sober."

We started walking and turned right, heading west on Lexington and into another cluster of charming historic homes that mirrored the ones on the east side, where Aunt Izzy's house was located. "Does he get drunk a lot?"

"Nope. That's why yesterday was so out of character, and why it makes me think there is more to the story."

"Do we have even have a story yet?"

"We know Connie was murdered, and either Chief Bennett or Lorraine did it. I'm wondering if perhaps they were secret

146

lovers, although the mere thought makes my skin crawl. Lorraine does go for power, but she likes smart power, and Bennett is a dolt. But if they had hooked up, they needed Connie out of the way if they wanted to be together."

"Killing someone is not the only way out of a marriage. There's this thing called divorce. Very trendy right now, especially with the Hollywood set."

"The *D* word would not be an option to someone of the Littletons' social status. One or the other would become an outcast as their friends took sides, most often in favor of the least culpable. In this case, if Lorraine were being unfaithful, she'd be tarred, feathered, escorted to the town limits, and tossed out like three-month-old garbage. Like I said, her position in town defined her. She would never leave. Never ever. Not in a million years. I'm hoping Max will shed some light on that subject."

"And Aunt Izzy?"

"I'm wondering if maybe she interrupted a secret midnight rendezvous down at the lighthouse, and one of them silenced her. After all, you found the oar in Lorraine's backyard, so putting two and two together, I think they may have killed Mizizzy too."

" 'They' being Lorraine and Chief Bennett?"

"Uh-huh."

The thought saddened me. Being beaten to death for being at the wrong place at the wrong time was worse than any diabolical premeditated killing I'd ever heard about. I held out hope she was killed defending a grand and noble cause. "Where does Mayor Twiddy come into the picture?"

"He doesn't." Sam sighed. A long sigh indicated I'd stretched her patience about as far as it was going to go. "You don't know Mayor Twiddy. We grew up together. He was two years ahead of me in school, the most popular boy ever to graduate from Braddocks Beach High. I know he was at Miami University when Chief Bennett claimed that, ah, lady-of-the-evening was killed. His diploma is hanging on the wall of his office. Mayor

Twiddy is as good and loyal and upstanding as they come. He doesn't so much as jaywalk in town. Not a speeding ticket to his name. Never missed a Sunday morning in the CDSE choir loft. He's squeaky clean. I'd bet my life on it. I just can't figure out Chief Bennett's motive for pointing the finger at Mayor Twiddy."

Sam stopped at a black wrought-iron gate and flicked the lever, granting us access to a well-kept but uninspired yard. Not an annual or perennial to offer a splash of color against the row of boxwoods that circled the front porch. I guessed the owner wasn't a member of the garden club.

We trip-tropped up the flagstone walkway, climbed the steps, and marched right through the front door as if we owned the place. We didn't get more than three steps in before we found a lifeless body lying facedown on the Persian runner in the entryway.

Sam stepped over Max as if he were a regurgitated fur ball and disappeared behind a door under the stairs. I studied the body for signs of life. A gentle rise and fall assured me he was still breathing. I raised my finger to my nose to stem the stench of recycled Dewar's.

Sam returned a moment later carrying a bowl filled with water. She stepped toward Max and stopped when the tips of her shoes touched the top of his head. With a flick of her wrist, the contents of the bowl showered Max. He groaned, but that was about it.

Sam leaned over and grabbed a handful of Max's brown hair, lifted his head, and let it drop back to the floor. Nose first. Another groan.

"Come on, Max. Time to wake up. We need some answers from you." Sam poked him with her foot, but still nothing. "Help me out, will you, Ellery? Let's get him to the kitchen and get some coffee in him."

Sam and I were both huffing and puffing by the time we got him set up in a chair at the kitchen table. His upper body lay splayed across the glass tabletop, his backside in a café-style chair that slid away from the table in accordance with Newton's law of gravity. My job was to brace my foot on the chair leg to prevent Max from ending up on the floor. We'd expended too much energy to get him off it.

Sam fixed coffee. Instant. Three cups in the microwave at once, bless her soul. While the water heated, she tried again to rouse Max by slapping his face. He became alert enough to tell us to go away and leave him alone. Only he didn't put it quite that nicely.

"Come on, Max. Just a few questions, then we'll leave. You can sleep all day," Sam said in a tired voice.

The microwave dinged, indicating the water zapping had finished. Sam turned her attention to dumping spoonfuls of instant crystals into the mugs while I kept my foot braced against the chair. I thought this a lost cause and planned to suggest we come back in a few hours, but not until after I'd had some coffee.

Sam fixed mine with cream and double sugar without even asking. I appreciated the effort but would have taken it straight at this point.

I stood and sipped while Sam sat and stared. At Max. So much for the tantalizing scent of coffee to bring him out of his stupor.

My leg started to cramp from being in the same flexed position, and I wondered if Sam planned to sit there and wait for Max to wake up. That could be hours. Maybe days. I tossed back the rest of my coffee and slammed the mug on the table.

"Hey. Great idea."

"What?"

"We need to make some noise." Sam popped out of her chair and started opening and closing cupboards. She knelt down in front of a corner cabinet and spun the lazy Susan around until she found two copper-bottomed pans. She handed me one, along with a long-handled wooden spoon snagged from the utensil jar on the counter. "And a one anna two anna one two three."

We banged the spoons against the pots, making enough noise to wake the dead. And with a little more enthusiasm, we managed to rouse Max.

"What the hell?" he sputtered groggily and lifted his head a fraction of an inch off the table. "Stop that! Stop that god-damn noise!"

"Good morning, Max."

"Sam? What the hell are you doing here?" His words slurred a bit, whether from sleep or leftover liquor, I couldn't be sure.

"We have a few questions for you."

"Okay, but lower your voice a few notches, will you?" Max lifted his head and cradled it between his hands. Sam lifted the mug to his lips and let him drink.

"Oh, gawd. What did I do?"

"No word of you dancing naked through the streets."

"I just wanna sleep—" His head dropped forward.

Sam grabbed him by his crown and lifted it back up. "Not until you answer a few questions for us first."

"About what?"

"About Connie and Lorraine. And how she's left penniless."

"Who told you that?"

"You told Ellery last night."

"Oh, gawd."

"Now how, in a state that has gone over the moon to protect spouses' rights, did Connie manage to take everything away from Lorraine?"

"Attorney-client privilege," he mumbled.

Sam looked at me and I looked at her. At her nod, we both took up our instruments and started banging for all we were worth. The noise gave me a headache. It must have been hell on someone with a hangover.

Max held up his hand in surrender. His eyes squinched in pain. "A trust. Are you happy? Connie convinced Lorraine to move everything to a trust, including the house, under the pre-text of a tax advantage so that Cordy wouldn't be burdened with a huge inheritance tax. And once it was set up, it took only one signature, Connie's, to move everything out. He knew he couldn't take it with him if he died first, so this was the only way he could make sure she didn't receive one red cent."

That left Sam speechless, which left Max looking a bit happier. Which left me wondering one thing. "Why?" I asked.

When Max didn't answer right away, Sam picked up her wooden spoon. Max reached his hand out and snatched it away from her. "You two missed your calling. You should be interrogating terrorists."

"I can't save the world, Max. But I can find out who killed Mizizzy and Connie. So start talking."

"Connie was killed?" That seemed to rouse Max more than the bowl of water had.

"Yes. Now please tell me why he squirreled away all their money before I go dig out your trumpet and start serenading you with Reveille."

"Because Lorraine had been unfaithful."

"Do you know with whom?"

Max started to shake his head, but then seemed to think better of the quick motion. "No. He knew, but he never told me. Said that part wasn't important."

"Do you think it could have been Chief Bennett?"

Max turned his head and stared at Sam as if she'd just sprouted butterfly wings. "The chief? Can't see that happening."

Sam turned and walked across the tiled floor, apparently in think mode. She opened the cupboard above the sink and took down a bottle of Tylenol. Flipping the lid, she poured a generous helping into her hand and replaced the bottle. She popped some in her mouth and tossed her head back, swallowing them without benefit of water. Returning to the table, she laid three gel caps in front of Max, who had his elbows on the table and his head propped between his hands. "You've been very helpful, Max. Very helpful. Sorry to have troubled you this morning."

She jerked her head toward the back door and we turned to leave. Just as I placed my hand on the doorknob, Sam spoke again. "One more question, Max. Did you know about Betty Anne being related to Connie?"

But Max had already slipped to the floor in an unconscious heap. "Good," Sam said as she turned to leave. "I doubt he'll even remember our visit."

Chapter Twenty-four

We made our away along an alley that snaked between what had originally been carriage houses to the larger, more ornate homes on the main road. With no horses or buggies to shelter, the small buildings had been converted to dwellings.

"So now what?" Sam asked.

"Sleep." My synapses synapsed faster when I was fully rested. I was so tired right now, I'd be hard pressed to rattle off my name, rank, and Social Security number if asked, even if a bayonet was pressing against my windpipe.

"I'd be afraid to close my eyes right now, with Chief Bennett still on the loose, wouldn't you?"

I hadn't thought about that. "We could go to a hotel somewhere far away." Yes, far, far away from this craziness. Someplace where I hadn't been accused of murder, hadn't been tied to a chair and left to rot, and didn't have to torture people to get information. A place I could sleep without fear of waking up with the fishes.

"Let's go to Flossie's, grab something to snack on. We'll find a bench in the park, sit, and talk through what we know. We have so many little puzzle pieces that just don't seem to fit together at all."

"Maybe we're working on two separate puzzles."

"Maybe."

I got the impression Sam didn't buy into that theory. I didn't really, either. This town was too small for two murders in two weeks that weren't somehow intertwined.

The church bells *bong*ed eight times, calling people to worship.

153

Our pace slowed as we reentered the tourist district, the crowds having increased significantly in the past hour. Judging by the line that stretched from Reba's and along the next three storefronts, they all seemed to be in search of breakfast. Lucky skunks.

Flossie's Pharmacy was a peaceful haven. It was too early for souvenir-shopping tourists or prescription-filling townies, so we were the only customers in the store.

"Morning, Flossie," Sam said and introduced me to the young woman with one long, thick-as-my-wrist chestnut braid pulled over the shoulder of her white lab coat.

"Can Viagra be deadly?" Sam asked without benefit of small talk.

"There are always risks when taking any medication, but the chances increase exponentially with Viagra if it is mixed with other drugs, like nitroglycerin."

Sam inhaled sharply. "How so?"

"They each work their magic by lowering blood pressure. Taken in unison, the blood pressure drops so low the person can die."

Sam nodded. The faint squeaking sound I heard could have come from the cogs twisting and turning in her brain. Or my shoe against the sparkling linoleum floor as I shifted my weight to size up the snack section for my morning repast.

"I know Connie occasionally took nitroglycerin for his heart, but he didn't strike me as the type to need a little purple pill to help him in the bedroom," Sam said.

"What are you getting at? That Connie died of a drug inter-action?"

"Let's just say we have credible information that he did. We're investigating the source of the Viagra. How many prescriptions did you fill for it here?"

"Who died and appointed you two as chief detectives?" Flossie's tone of voice was half joking, half irritated. And half in bad taste, considering the recent rash of deaths.

"We're self-appointed after having been held hostage in Chief Bennett's cabin last night." Sam filled Flossie in on the basics, only untruthful in that she referred to Mayor Twiddy as an unnamed suspect.

Flossie's eyes grew rounder with each event, interjecting every other sentence with "Get out!"

"So we're trying to narrow down our suspects by finding out who might have had access to Viagra," Sam concluded. "I'm thinking you have only a handful of customers."

"You'd be surprised. Half the male population over the age of forty-five takes a drug to overcome erectile dysfunction. But I can tell you honestly that Connie Littleton was not one of them. Well, at least not from my pharmacy."

"Did Chief Bennett have a prescription filled here?"

"I can only tell you who didn't. Telling you who did would be breaking client-pharmacist privileges."

Sam repeated her question. Flossie's nonanswer told us all we needed to know.

"Did Mayor Twiddy?" I ducked as the last few words left my lips, because it looked as if Sam was going to smack me. But it was a question that needed asking, if only to eliminate him for my own peace of mind.

Again, no answer. We thanked her for her help, loaded up on Chips Ahoy snack packs, cold orange juice, and a Hello Kitty notepad and matching pen from the clearance rack by the front door. Sam had everything put on my tab, and we headed outside for breakfast in the park.

"What do you think?" Sam asked.

"Professor Plum with the lead pipe in the billiard room."

"I'm serious. I know we have more questions than answers, but I can't help but feel we're very, very close to finding out who killed Mizizzy and Connie." Sam took out the pen and began scribbling. I sipped my juice.

"Let's start with what we do know. Mizizzy was killed in the watchtower in the late night hours on May thirtieth. Death by a boat-oar beating."

I shivered at the thought.

"Connie was killed on June eleventh by a Viagra slipped into his chicken salad that combined with his nitroglycerin. We just don't know who slipped it there. Could have been Lorraine or Bennett."

I thought about how tired and aged Connie had looked when I'd last seen him alive, walking away from Sam's garage after arranging to meet me the next day to share his and Aunt Izzy's secret project. I wondered if the drug combination had already begun to affect him. Was there something I could have, should have, done to save his life? Guilt washed over me, giving rise to a new resolve to find the murderer. Maybe it was the same person who'd killed Aunt Izzy. But why? I sat up taller in my seat, forcing myself to concentrate on the puzzle before us.

"Connie left Lorraine destitute because she'd had an extramarital affair. Or maybe still was having? Hmmm. Connie and Mizizzy had a secret that only they knew, and Mizizzy suspected Connie had a biological sister in Betty Anne and had ordered the DNA testing." Sam flipped to a blank page on the tablet. "What we don't know is why or by whom either was killed, what their secret project was, where Lorraine slept the night Connie died, or whom Lorraine was talking about when she said, 'We'll have to kill him.'"

"I forgot to tell you Doodles told me last night that Doris misspoke. It wasn't Lorraine, but someone else he'd overheard. But Pipsqueak attacked the food table at that time, and we didn't have an opportunity to finish our conversation."

Sam's ears wiggled, which I took for a sign her head was about to explode. I scooted to the end of the bench.

"When were you going to tell me that?"

I shrugged my shoulders. I'd forgotten about it myself.

"So that takes Lorraine off the top of my list of suspects."

"That and the fact that Connie was worth more to her alive than dead, considering she doesn't have a house or money or livelihood now."

"Good point. But did she know that?"

Sam flipped to a new page. "If she did think that Connie and Betty Anne were doing the horizontal mamba like she accused at my potluck dinner, maybe it was a moment of jealousy. Or hope. She would have cause to divorce him and come out as the injured party."

"Or, as Chief Bennett said, Mayor Twiddy killed Connie. Maybe the mayor was having an affair with Lorraine and wanted Connie out of the way? If she wouldn't divorce him, like you said, maybe it was a crime of passion?"

Sam shook her head violently, then seemed to think better of it as she laid her hand against her injury. "Never in a million years would those two get together. If it weren't for good breeding, those two would be tearing each other's eyes out every time they crossed paths. They hate each other. A grudge going back to high school. Nobody's quite sure why, though."

Love and hate are the two closest-related emotions. I thought about the flirtatious look I had seen Lorraine give Mayor Twiddy at the potluck but held my tongue. The darkness and the distance could have played a trick on my eyes. Sam knew these people better than I did. "I still think Mayor Twiddy is our prime suspect," I said. "I won't rest easy until Officer Compton hauls him down for questioning."

"You don't know Mayor Twiddy the way I do. He would never kill anyone." Sam drew some curlicues on her notepad.

"Chief Bennett said Mayor Twiddy killed that girl many years ago. It's feasible something set him off again. Maybe something inside him snapped."

"You believe that lying scumball Chief Bennett over our esteemed and trustworthy Mayor Twiddy?"

Put that way, I wasn't so sure.

"I can't help but think the connection has something to do with the DNA test results," I said.

"Maybe Betty Anne can shed some light on the subject."

I doubted it, but I felt I needed to be doing something constructive, or I might go crazy.

"If the killer hasn't struck again, that is," Sam said.

"What makes you say that?" I shivered, as if a ghost had just walked across my grave.

"I'm just thinking like a killer." Sam shrugged her shoulders. "And if the motive for killing *was* to prevent the Cordy/Fitz-Two relationship from being revealed, then he will need to make sure everyone who knows is silenced."

"We don't know that Betty Anne knows—"

"I'm thinking that's why she was seen leaving the Littletons' house on the night of your welcome-to-the-neighborhood potluck. Connie might have told her he suspected it."

"Pure conjecture."

"No. Part conjecture, part intuition. We can ask her, though. I just saw her car go by. She's probably on her way to the nine-thirty church service. Come on." Sam stood.

A thought managed to wiggle its way from the deepest recesses of my mind. "Whoever took the DNA letter from Aunt Izzy's house might think we know too."

"That means we might be on the top of the killer's Next-to-Be-Killed list ourselves. I told you we should have purchased a gun at Big-Mart."

I kind of wished I'd listened to her.

Chapter Twenty-five

Betty Anne," Sam called to the woman dressed in a daiquiri-colored freedom-fabric suit with a two-shades-darker blouse. The woman walked, hunched over, in the manner of a basset hound with its nose on the trail. "Do you have a minute?"

"Any chance it can wait until after services?" Betty Anne turned her head and pushed a stray strand of black hair that had escaped her tight bun, enabling me to catch a glimpse of smooth skin and a troubled smile.

Sam and I fell into step alongside her. The pace settled somewhere between a trot and a gallop as we hurried along the long sidewalk leading to the church's front doors, swung wide open to saints and sinners alike.

"I'm filling in for Scootch," Betty Anne said. "She got the call that Arabella's water broke, so she raced off to Sandusky. The birth of the first grandchild is such a blessed event. I'm hoping to get a few minutes before the service to run through the new arrangement of 'Live Like You Were Dying.' Reverend Hammersmith selected it to follow his message today. I guess Connie's and Miss Izzy's deaths so close to each other have hit the congregation pretty hard. Today's sermon is going to double as grief counseling."

The reminder of two deaths already, with ours possibly soon to follow, left a bowling-ball-size of dread in my belly. I glanced over my shoulder, fully expecting to see the muzzle of an Uzi pointing at us through the lavender chintz curtains in the six-over-six window of the white Victorian across the street, or a pack of thugs armed with brass knuckles and baseball bats stepping out from behind the oak trees that offered shade along the street. Braddocks Beach took on a sinister aura, in that an evil feeling seemed to be piggybacking on rays of sunshine. I felt cold and hot at the same time.

The sound of a car backfiring startled me. I turned to look. My foot caught on an uneven slab of cement and caused me to stumble. Momentum carried me forward, and I fell to the ground, taking Sam and Betty Anne with me like they were my football tackling dummies.

Just as we landed in the bed of petunias, another explosive sound blasted from the street, which was echoed by the sound of shattering glass. Betty Anne screamed.

Sam shouted, "Get down" and then poked her own head up to survey the area.

It registered in my brain that it had been a gunshot and not a car backfiring, since cars don't even backfire in this age of unleaded gas. I just lay there, a puddle of quivering, shivering nerves. Someone had just shot at us. Someone was trying to kill us. I surveyed my body. No gaping holes. No gushing blood. He'd missed.

Officer Compton raced toward us. "Did you get a look at the car?" he asked.

"It was Chief Bennett." Sam collapsed flat on her back in the grass, gulping air.

"You saw him?"

"No, I saw his truck."

"But not him?"

"Nope."

"Which way did he go?"

"West on Boston Street."

"I'll get an APB out." Officer Compton turned and galloped across the church's front lawn toward the police station, all the time his gaze sweeping the area as if looking for additional snipers. The thought that the shooter might double back and try again had me scrambling for the protection of the bushes along the church's foundation. I sure hoped the delicate white flowers on a gardenia branch could offer me safety against another bullet.

The Westminster chimes rang the half hour. Being right under the steeple, their cacophony made my heart rumble in my chest. Or maybe I was having a heart attack. I couldn't be sure.

Betty Anne's screams dwindled to whimpers, then started up in anguish. I looked at her and saw her staring at something above my head. I looked up to see that all that was left of a large, stained-glass window were a few shards of colorful glass protruding from the edges. My trembling worsened, and I concentrated on trying to hold my head still so that it didn't pop off, because my insides felt like a bottle of champagne that had been shaken. That window could have been one of us. It could have been me.

"You saved our lives, El," Sam said. "You're a hero."

Me, a hero? Didn't that require an act of unselfish bravery? All I'd done was trip and fall. Pure, clumsy luck. I'd have said as much too, if I could've gotten my mouth to work.

Two police cars screeched to a stop on the street, their red-and-blue pulsing lights adding confusion to the scene. Four police officers jumped out and swarmed the area. "Officer Compton wants to talk to you, so please don't go anywhere," one said to us as he bound up the stairs into the church.

Now why hadn't I thought of that?

I'm sure we would have received more attention if we'd been injured, but we were no worse for the wear. Well, Betty Anne's panty hose were torn at the knees, and Sam's cheek had a seeping scrape, but there were no deadly gunshot wounds. Guess it wasn't our time to go. Not yet, anyway. But the events of the day had to have taken a few years off my life. I pressed my fingers to my temples in an attempt to ease the building pressure. It didn't help. Not one bit.

"I wonder who just tried to kill us," Sam whispered as she rolled me to a semi-sitting position.

"I thought you said it was Chief Bennett," Betty Anne said, her whisper hissing with fear.

"He's a trained marksman. Don't you think he would have hit us if he wanted to?"

I shuddered. There was just something so surreal about

sitting here, bathed in the glorious sunlight and the aura of the church, talking about our near-death experience.

"I think somebody else was driving his car. I wish I'd seen who."

Sam and Betty Anne stood and brushed petals from each other's backs. My legs weren't working yet, so it was all I could do to prop myself up against the church steps. My heart rate slowed as the adrenaline rush wore off, leaving me even more tired than before. I didn't think that was possible.

The sun hung directly over Sam and Betty Anne's heads, and I couldn't see their faces without squinting, which aggravated the headache pounding at my temples. I focused instead on Betty Anne's seamless-stockinged toes peeking out the tip of her sandals and listened while they talked.

"Why is someone trying to kill you two?" Betty Anne asked.

"I think you may have been the target," Sam said.

"Me?" Betty Anne's toes retracted into the safety of her white vinyl sandals, turtle-style. I wish I had a protective shell I could pull myself into.

"Did Connie tell you about the results of the DNA test?"

"You think that had something to do with the shooting spree?" Betty Anne asked.

"I'm pretty sure. So you know?"

"Yes, but how do you know? Did he tell you?"

"Yes." It never ceased to amaze me how easily lies rolled off Sam's tongue. "But he didn't have time to tell me all the details. When did he tell you?"

"The night of the potluck at your house. He'd asked me to stop by on my way over and told me then."

Sam's theory was confirmed. "How did he get a sample without you knowing?" she asked.

"My dentist and he were fraternity brothers. At my last cleaning, Doctor Brightwell took a cheek swab, and Connie sent our samples to the lab. He said he didn't have the written reports yet, but expected them to arrive at Izzy's house any day. He didn't want Lorraine to get suspicious. Anyway, he'd received a phone call with the verbal results. But I don't see the connection between that and someone wanting to kill me."

While I wondered at the ethics of taking a cheek swab without someone's permission, Sam went through the whole Cordy/Fitz-Two first-cousins theory. Betty Anne seemed to buy into the idea that that would be a motive for murder, but she couldn't see Lorraine in the role of the killer. I guess I didn't understand the social hierarchy of Braddocks Beach, because it just seemed too bizarre to put social status over human life.

"Are you full-blood or half-blood siblings?" Sam asked.

"Full-blood."

"How did that happen?"

"All I know from Connie is that Bass Littleton wasn't Connie's biological father." I watched Betty Anne's toes relax, and she shuffled her feet. "Some traveling salesman was, as Connie discovered when he found his mother's diary hidden in the attic. Shortly after Connie's birth, Bass was involved in an accident that left him unable to sire any more children, common knowledge around town. So when Victoria found herself pregnant again, by the same salesman, she went to visit an ailing aunt in Vermont for six months, gave birth, and gave the baby up for adoption. That baby was me."

"How did Connie find out about your existence?" Sam asked.

"He said it was a long and expensive search," Betty Anne said. "Called it his secret project. Part of a citywide genealogical project he and Izzy were working on. He hinted that more than one of our esteemed ancestors played in someone else's sandbox, if you get my drift."

Sam nodded, then asked, "Don't you think it's ironic that you met Fitz-One in college and ended up back here?"

"Serendipity, that's for sure. This place felt like home from the first step I took on Tinsdale Street when we'd come for a visit," Betty explained. "We never left. The minute we passed the WELCOME sign, I felt like I belonged here. Now I understand why. It's in my blood."

Talk ceased as the police asked us to move so they could

secure the crime scene with yellow tape. I guess we were far enough north from the tourist district that it wasn't necessary to keep up appearances the way they'd done after Aunt Izzy's murder.

Sam and Betty Anne helped me to my feet, and we walked to the end of the sidewalk. We stopped in the no-man's-land between the crime scene and the looky-loos. The way they stared, you'd think none of them had ever seen a drive-by shooting.

"Do you know if Mizizzy knew any of this?" Sam asked in a low voice.

Betty Anne nodded.

"Anyone else?"

"Connie said we needed to keep this all quiet for now."

"But what about Cordy and Fitz-Two being first cousins? Certainly, they couldn't go through with the marriage. Their children—"

Betty Anne held her finger up to shush Sam before she could finish the dire prediction. "Connie said he needed to do more research, that there was more to this than met the eye. We had to be sure. Those two are so much in love. Do you realize what this would do to them? Fitz-Two would be devastated. Cordy is the love of his life, his soul mate. His reason for living."

Officer Compton, looking beyond stressed, joined our group. "I'll need you to make an official statement," he said with authority. "Let's go to the station where we can talk." He nodded toward the growing crowd, primarily parishioners dressed in their best Sunday go-to-meetin' clothes. I saw a few faces I recognized—Reba, Mystic, Veralee, Flossie, Zanna, Merry Sue—and a few more nameless ones from Friday night's barbecue.

As we made our way across the soggy fescue toward the east side of the sprawling municipal center, I started sneezing. Big, three-ahs-before-a-choo sneezes. I must be allergic to fresh air. Or stress. Betty Anne passed me a Kleenex, bless her heart, as my tunic didn't have sleeves long enough to reach my nose.

Back under the glaring lights of the interrogation room and

the assessing glare of Officer Compton, Betty Anne gave her account of the events. For the record, she said she'd been on her way to church for a last-minute run-through when she'd met up with us, been thrown to the ground, and had her life spared due to the quick actions of me. She broke down in tears as she patted my hand and thanked me over and over and over. The more I protested, the more she insisted she owed her life to me. I stopped before things digressed to ridiculous.

Officer Compton let Betty Anne go at 8:53, and she took off for the church. The show must go on.

For the second time in less than two hours, Sam and I gave signed official statements.

"Do you want police protection?" Officer Compton asked.

"No," Sam said.

I still suffered from a sudden drop in adrenaline and couldn't get my mouth to work to contradict her. There was something to be said for the safety of the cement walls of the police station, to be sure.

Sam stood, although she appeared be a bit wobbly to my eyes, or maybe it was just my eyes that were wobbly. "I'm sure it's safe enough for us to walk home. It's a beautiful morning, there are police everywhere, and we'll lock ourselves inside Mizizzy's house and not answer the door for anyone. I think all we want to do is sleep."

"In my professional opinion, that shooter is long gone by now. It should be safe to go home. As soon as the next shift arrives, I'll send someone over to keep an eye on the house."

"I'd appreciate that. Come on, El, let's go."

We rose and made our way outside. It was, indeed, a gorgeous day.

"Ya know something?" Sam asked as we strolled side by side down the sidewalk.

"What?"

"Since Connie is out of the way, Lorraine is free to marry Chief Bennett."

"He's leaving the country in a few hours. From what you told me, she'd never leave this town."

"Not willingly, but if her hands were as dirty as his, she wouldn't have a choice." Her voice trailed off.

"You still think that Lorraine is behind all this?"

"I'm more sure than ever."

"Any chance she was the one driving the car?"

"I'd bet my life on it."

In light of recent events, I wasn't so quick to bet my life on anything.

Chapter Twenty-six

I saw Aunt Izzy's house at the end of the street, glittering like a beacon in the morning sun. The sight made my heart skip a little with something that felt like pride. I quickened my pace. I was so close to being able to lay my head down that I allowed my eyelids to droop until I could see just enough sidewalk to lead me home.

But two driveways short of my destination, Sam grabbed me by the elbow and spun me in the direction of the Littletons'. So close, and yet so far. "Now what?" Had that whiny voice come from my mouth?

"I need to check something out. Show me where you found that oar."

With a heavy sigh intended to show my displeasure, and an equally heavy sigh from Sam indicating her annoyance at my lack of enthusiasm, I dragged myself down the driveway to the spot behind the garage. I stopped and pointed. The leaves had been raked away, probably by the police looking for additional clues, leaving only mud. Plain, brown mud. Sam dropped to her knees and studied the ground. "Were these footprints here last night?"

"How should I know? It was covered by leaves."

"Come here and look."

Figuring that the quicker we got this over with, the quicker I'd get to bed, I dropped to my knees and looked along with her. Faint tracks led the entire length of the garage and back again. A few times—indicating not just a casual shortcut, but a determined pacing, as if looking for something. I found one clear, solitary print outside the rest, and bent close enough that

I could smell the wet, wormy earth. The footprint left a very definitive imprint, with a distinctive zigzag tread pattern. "What kind of shoes do the boys in blue wear around here?" I asked.

"Black boots. Why?"

"Because these tracks were made by Docksiders. I know, because I had a husband who used to wear them and refused to take them off when he came in from the backyard. He left footprints all across my kitchen floor. Do many men wear boat shoes around here?"

Sam gave me a puzzled look.

"They're slip-on shoes, brown leather with lighter stitching and a lighter rubber sole. They're the preferred footwear of yachtsmen."

"We don't have any yachts on Lake Braddock, let alone any yachtsmen."

I remembered seeing a pair of boat shoes recently. Just last night, come to think of it. "The kind of shoes Doodles wears."

"Oh."

I waited for Sam's thoughts to catch up to mine.

"Oh!" Sam said. "You think Doodles was back here?"

"I say it's worth asking a few questions."

Sam was off the ground and racing down the driveway in the blink of an eye. "Come on," she called over her shoulder. I rose and followed suit, crossing my fingers that this wouldn't take very long.

Finding him didn't, as we intercepted him on his way back up the sidewalk, newspaper in hand. He sported a cozy, grape-colored terrycloth robe, no shirt underneath. It didn't bear thinking about whether or not he wore boxers. The robe stopped just below the knee, exposing pale, spindly legs that dipped down into the shoes in question.

"Oh, Doodles," Sam called in a cheery voice.

Doodles stopped scanning the headlines and glanced in our direction. "Morning, Sam. Ellery." Doodle's voice was not as cheery. In fact, it sounded downright hostile.

But Sam was a woman with a mission, and it would take more than a surly greeting to knock her off course. "We were wondering if you could do us a favor."

Doodles glanced toward his front door, as if gauging his chances of making it inside and locking it before Sam and I could catch up with him.

"That lightbulb above Mizizzy's kitchen table has gone out again," Sam continued, "and we were hoping you could change it for us."

"Now?"

By this point, we had him surrounded. "Now!" Sam ordered, grabbing him by the upper arm and spinning him around. I grabbed the other arm, and we frog-marched Doodles across the street. The dropped newspaper caught the gentle lake breeze and scattered across the front lawn like confetti.

As we entered Aunt Izzy's kitchen, Sam flicked the switch and the light over the kitchen table illuminated as bright as you please.

"There's nothing wrong with the bulb," Doodles said, a master of the obvious.

"You're right. We have a few questions for you. Please, have a seat."

"I don't have anything to tell you."

"But I think you do. Sit." Sam shoved a kitchen chair into the back of Doodles' knees, and he sat. She walked around front and held out her hand. "Shoe."

"What?"

"I need to see your shoe." Doodles shrugged his shoulders, then crossed his right foot over his left knee, slipped his Docksider off, and handed it over. Sam studied the distinctive tread, and then handed it to me. "What do you think?"

I inspected it closely, noticing the dried mud packed tight in the zigzag crevices, and nodded.

"Sneaking around behind Lorraine's shed, huh?" I asked.

"What are you getting at?"

"If it's bluntness you want, it's bluntness you'll get." Sam placed her fists on her hips and bent down until she was nose to nose with Doodles. "You're having an affair with Lorraine Littleton."

"What?" both Doodles and I cried in unison.

"How else can you explain your footprints behind her garage?"

Sam had added two plus two and come up with ninety-nine. I was willing to bet my life that Doodles and Lorraine were nothing more than nodding neighbors. But there was sweat on his brow, and his breath came in shallow, rapid hisps. This man was guilty of something, and my money was on Sam to wriggle it out of him. I moved in closer so I could gauge both sides of the inquisition.

Doodles started to fidget. "I don't have to answer any of your questions. You're not the police. In fact, I think I'll leave." He started to rise. Sam pushed him back down.

"We can make this easy, or we can make this hard. What's your choice?"

"Sam," Doodles pleaded. "How long have we known each other? Twenty years? How can you accuse me of something so preposterous?"

"I've learned over the past few days that I don't know my neighbors as well as I thought." Sam settled back on her heels, crossed her arms, and stared Doodles down. "So what were you doing sneaking around the Littletons' garage?"

Doodles pressed his lips so tightly together they turned white. Then blue. His hands were clenched at his sides, but he didn't make eye contact with either of us. He was hiding something.

"Ellery," Sam said in a melodic voice. "Could you be so kind as to grab that *Death by Chocolate* cookbook off the top of the refrigerator, please?"

Aunt Izzy had organized her cookbooks in decreasing size from left to right. The requested tome was smack-dab in the middle. I retrieved it, and took one long, wistful look at the cover before handing it to Sam. "Unless he's diabetic, it's not possible to actually kill someone with too much chocolate. If it were, I'd have been gone a long time ago."

Sam took the book from my hands and flipped to the inside cover, where she extracted a photo. One from the early 1960s or so, I thought, based on its four-by-four size and the white border around the black-and-white print. She flipped it around so that Doodles could see it.

I had thought that people "blanching" was just a figure of speech, but the way Doodles' face went from mad-as-a-hornet red to overcooked-egg-noodle white made me a believer. Something in that photo had him scared.

How bad could a picture be?

Inquiring minds wanted to know.

I maneuvered until I stood behind him and could see the small Kodak photo. There was no doubt the striped-shirt-, wrinkled-shorts-, and sagging-socks-wearing boy in that picture was a young Doodles. Nor was there any doubt that the salt and vinegar he was pouring over Aunt Izzy's roses was intended to kill them.

"The great rose-icide incident of '71. You ruined more than a dozen gardens throughout the town, including the one at City Hall. There's still a bounty on your head."

Doodles licked his lips, his gaze darting from the picture to Sam and back again.

"Mizizzy kept your secret for over twenty-five years. If it came out now, you would not only be stripped of your title as president of the Braddocks Beach Rose Society, but I bet they'd yank your master gardener's certificate, and maybe burn that collection of blue ribbons hanging in your greenhouse."

"What do you want?" Doodles' voice sounded like his vocal chords had been rubbed with sandpaper.

"The picture gets destroyed, if you answer a few questions."

He nodded and reached for the photo.

Sam pulled it away. "Answers first. Why were you sneaking behind the Littletons' garage?"

"It all goes back to the night Miss Izzy died. I'd heard voices, as Doris told you. A woman said, 'One of us is going to have to kill him.' Only it wasn't Lorraine, like she thought."

"Why did you tell Doris it was?" Sam asked.

"I didn't. She jumped to that conclusion on her own. I wasn't sure who was talking until I heard them again, at Miss Izzy's funeral."

"Who was it?" I asked, leaning in closer.

"The voices were Zanna Wilson and Mayor Twiddy." He reached for the photo, but I was quicker on the draw and snatched it out of Sam's hand so I could safely guard it. Sam would be no match for Doodles, should he decide to wrestle her for it. I, on the other hand, felt confident I'd win the battle of the bulge against my round neighbor.

"What did they say at the funeral?" I asked.

"Something about killing someone who knew too much."

"Him, not her." I wanted to be perfectly clear on this item. Doodles nodded.

"Is that all you heard?" I waved the picture in front of him.

Doodles' shoulders slumped. His eyelids slipped over weary eyes, and he took a deep breath. "I kind of, uh, happened to be hiding under a coat in the back of the mayor's SUV after the funeral. Zanna and Twiddy got in and had a private discussion. I learned they'd been having an affair for years."

Sam inhaled so sharply she choked. I glanced in her direction, then quickly grabbed a kitchen chair and slid it behind her before she hit the floor.

"The two had colluded to skim money from the city, more than a million dollars," Doodles continued, accompanied by Sam's exclamations of incredulity. "They had a system where Zanna drew up fake invoices for payment, Twiddy signed them, and the money went to a Swiss bank account."

With Zanna's position as city treasurer, this was a perfect setup.

"This had been going on for over fifteen years. Only recently someone started asking questions. They didn't say who, just kept calling him 'he.' And they planned to kill him."

"I still don't get what this has to do with you sneaking around the Littletons' garage."

"Connie died so suddenly, I was suspicious. Could he have been the one they planned to murder?"

"It seems that way," I said. "The police are investigating it now. Your information could be very helpful. You need to talk to Officer Compton immediately."

Doodles screwed his eyes up and a tear dripped from the corner as his shoulders began to shake. "I should have gone to the police. Maybe Connie would still be alive if I had gone to the police. But I just thought . . . hoped . . . prayed it had been a heart attack. I know I should have gone about the embezzling, but I figured the audit would reveal it, and they would get caught, and I wouldn't get killed too." He'd dissolved into full, gut-wrenching sobs by that point.

I couldn't help but feel sorry for him. He'd lost two friends, too, and the blood of one of them, if not both, was on his hands. I walked to the stove and turned on the gas jets. Holding the incriminating evidence of Doodles' youthful vandalism, I watched as a flame caught the corner. It curled as it burned, then fell in a heap of ashes on the porcelain stovetop.

"What time did you hear this conversation, Doodles? The one from your bedroom window."

"Around midnight."

"What time was Aunt Izzy killed?" I asked Sam.

"Around midnight," she answered.

"So does anyone else think that Zanna and Twiddy might have killed Aunt Izzy too?"

Nobody seemed to have an answer to that one.

Chapter Twenty-seven

Doodles left to dress and call the police.

Sam paced the perimeter of Aunt Izzy's kitchen like a caged animal, twisting a calendar towel in her hands like she was a pioneer woman and it was a chicken to be cooked for Sunday supper. "Based on what Doodles just told us, Mayor Twiddy and/or Zanna killed Connie because he'd somehow learned of their skimming money from the city. I'm wondering if they also killed Mizizzy because she'd stumbled upon their midnight rendezvous down at the lighthouse. But how does Chief Bennett's car shooting at us fit into the picture?"

"And we still have Lorraine, remember. She didn't sleep at her house the night Connie died. If she was in on it and she knew someone was going to slip Connie a deadly purple pill—or maybe she did it herself—it's like she didn't want to be around to witness his slow and painful demise."

"Do you think it was slow and painful?" Sam's voice caught in her throat.

"I hope it wasn't."

"Me too." Silence hung heavy between us as we gave in to our thoughts.

Sam spoke first. "I guess we should go and tell Officer Compton what we think. Let him take it from there."

"I don't know what else we can do at this point."

"The sooner we go, the sooner they can haul Twiddy in for questioning."

Sam's omission of the mayoral title spoke volumes. It can't be easy to have a person you know and love and trust turn out to be a killer. "I'll drive," I said, not wanting to take the chance that Sam would rather walk.

We drove into town. "Pull over," Sam ordered as I entered Tinsdale Circle. She jumped out of the car before Bessie had even slowed to a stop in front of Hansel and Gretel's. I stayed put, the engine idling, contemplating the option of following her inside the crowded shop or closing my eyes for a quick catnap. The aroma of fresh fudge wafting from the gift-and-goodies shop made the decision easy.

The shop was crowded. Veralee was having a taste-testing party, and all manner of gourmet treats were being passed around on silver trays carried by young girls dressed in little Dutch-girl outfits complete with funny hats and wooden shoes. "Pâté de fois gras?" This offered by The Sheepdog herself. I couldn't refuse, she seemed so eager to please, but I was not a big fan. I smiled my thanks and popped it into my mouth but didn't chew. When Veralee turned her offerings on another customer, I spun around and spit it into my napkin, which I tucked into my pocket for as-soon-as-possible disposal. Another tray came by filled with mini crabmeat quiches, and I snagged three, enjoying every last savory bite.

I spotted Sam in the back corner talking to someone whose back was to me. I made my way in her direction, sampling sushi, mushroom croustades, and chocolate-covered strawberries as I went.

I didn't need an introduction, as Cordy was the spitting image of her mother—except for her mouth. She had fleshy lips, unlike Lorraine's pencil-thin ones. Connie's were thin too, come to think of it. I studied the young woman more closely. Cordy had brown eyes. Lorraine and Connie both had blue. Third-grade science. A simple Punnett square. Blue is the recessive gene. Two blue-eyed parents will always, always have blue-eyed children. I knew with sudden clarity that Cordy was not Connie's biological daughter. And I suspected that Connie knew it too. That's why he'd told Betty Anne there was more to this than met the eye. Only there wasn't. The eyes gave it away. I wondered how long he'd known, and why nobody had figured this out long before.

We left the shop, cucumber-sandwich triangles and baklava samples in hand. As soon as we were in the car, I broke my theory to Sam.

"That's the most absurd thing I've ever heard."

"Hadn't you ever noticed?"

"Cordy is the spitting image of her mother."

"Yes, but not her father. Can you tell me honestly you see a single one of Connie's features in his daughter?"

Sam sputtered, "I have pictures of Lorraine and Connie standing on the steps of their house the day they brought Cordy home from the hospital. Two prouder parents you have never seen. They'd been married for four years at that point, had been trying desperately to have a baby. And they did. They had Cordy. And nobody ever asked any questions."

"Well, it's time someone did."

"What are you saying?"

"I'm just wondering if that's another secret that might be worth killing for."

"You mean Lorraine may have killed Connie if he found out the truth?"

"Possibly, if you believe divorce wasn't an option for her. Proof that Connie was not the father of her baby could certainly be grounds, and if she knew that he knew she was currently having an affair, I'd say that divorce was not just an option, but a certainty. I doubt she knew he was squirreling the money away, though, because while divorce would force her to leave town, his death left her financially destitute."

"Damn it." Sam paused. "Damn it, damn it, damn it. How can we prove Connie's not the father?"

"A simple blood test."

"For blood type?"

"For DNA. But if we knew their blood types, we could narrow down the paternity. Too bad we don't have access to their blood donor cards or something."

"Yes, we do. Let's go."

I backed Bessie out of the parking spot, and Sam directed me to drive to the back of a strip mall about a mile northwest of town. The parking lot was empty. Discarded candy wrappers and empty soda bottles bordered the asphalt. The evil-sunshine feeling crept along my spine again. "Maybe we should go back and get our police escort."

"Don't be such a ninny. There isn't anyone around for miles."

"That's the scary part."

"We'll be in and out before anyone knows we're here. Besides, nobody will recognize your car. You haven't been here long enough."

Forty-six hours. Not that I was counting. "I'd feel better if someone at least knew where we were."

"But—"

I shifted Bessie into reverse and eased my foot off the brake.

"Okay, okay." Sam laid her hand on mine, and with her help Bessie was shifted back into park. "Give me your cell phone. I'll leave a message for George."

I retrieved my phone from Bessie's console and handed it to her.

She flipped it open and tapped in the number. "George, honey, Ellery and I stopped to pick up those flyers for next month's blood drive. I promised to deliver them to the library by this afternoon. We'll be home soon. Love ya." Sam flipped the phone shut and looked at me. "Happy?" she said while she tossed it, somewhat disgustedly, back into the console.

Appeased would be a better word. But the foreboding feeling remained strong. "Where are we?" I asked.

"The bloodmobile, only it's not mobile. There's no need to travel around. The locals stop by often enough to keep supplies up. I volunteer here every Thursday." Sam hopped out and hustled to one of the back doors. The red one. I followed. She pushed some numbers into the cipher lock and turned the knob. Once inside, she flicked the lights on and walked over to a file cabinet. Twenty-first-century technology had not seeped through these cinder block walls. Sam pulled out a handful of manila folders. "Cordy's blood type is B. Lorraine's is A. Connie's is O. What does that mean?"

I really didn't want to be the one to break Sam's vision of a perfect world. "There is no way that Connie is Cordy's father. He would have to be B or AB."

"Are you sure?" Sam's lip began to quiver.

I thought of Cordy's lips, thick and fleshy. It reminded me of someone else's lips. I flashed back to the creepy feeling I'd had when Mayor Twiddy had pressed his fleshy lips against the back of my hand. I hoped not. For Sam's sake. For Connie's sake. For Cordy's sake.

I began opening file cabinets, searching the T's, but no Twiddys to be found. Nothing under M for mayor. Think. Think. He'd introduced himself as Owen Twiddle Rock. No. Owen Twiddle Marble. No, but I felt for sure it was something hard and round, because I'd associated his eyes with his last name. They'd been small black pebbles. Hard as stones. Stone, that was it! I flipped to the S's and pulled out Owen T. Stone's file. My hands shook as I flipped to the front chart. Blood type B. Copy of driver's license—eye color, blue. A coincidence? Perhaps. But Mayor Twiddy just shot to the top of my suspects list.

"I'm sorry," I apologized to Sam and showed her the file. She shook her head in disbelief.

We now had enough evidence to take to Officer Compton. Lorraine Littleton had means, motive, and opportunity to kill her husband, possibly with the help of Mayor Twiddy.

We replaced the files and headed back out to Bessie. The evil-sunshine feeling was back, and so were the sneezes. Thank goodness for the stash of fast-food-restaurant napkins stuffed into my truck's glove compartment. I was going through them at the rate of one a second as we drove back into town.

"You must be allergic to something," Sam said, handing down her medical opinion.

"Yeah. Chasing killers."

"The only other time you sneezed was when we were in Zanna's office."

"And today after the drive-by shooting." Proof in my mind I was allergic to stressful situations.

Sam stared out the window. "Zanna was in the crowd we passed this morning when you sneezed, wasn't she?"

"Yeah, I guess." I sneezed again. And again. And again. I opened the window, hoping to air out whatever was causing this allergic reaction. Three more sneezes. It felt like someone was scratching a toilet brush down the back of my throat and tickling my eardrums with a feather.

"Any other times you've sneezed?"

"When they were loading you into the ambulance."

"Was Zanna there?"

"Come to think of it, she was."

"Are you thinking what I'm thinking?"

"I don't think so." The only thing I was thinking was that I'd be running out of napkins soon.

"I'm thinking that Zanna was in this car while we were in the bloodmobile office."

"And I'm still here."

My gaze jumped from the road to my rearview mirror, where I saw Zanna Wilson, Braddocks Beach treasurer, peering over the backseat from the cargo area. It wasn't the diabolical sneer on her face that scared the bejesus out of me, or the way she was dressed from head to toe in black, complete with a black scarf around her head. What scared me was the short, gunmetal-gray, snub-nosed barrel of a gun.

My only thought was that had I taken the heat for Aunt Izzy's murder, I'd be alive and well fed behind bars at the state penitentiary.

Chapter Twenty-eight

If you start to scream, I'll silence you," Zanna said, wiggling the gun in a motion that indicated her preferred method of silencing.

I don't think I could have screamed if I'd wanted to, because my lungs were frozen mid-inhale.

"Pay attention to the road, please. I don't want anyone to get hurt here." She chuckled to herself. "Clarification. I don't want *me* to get hurt here."

I dragged my eyes from the rearview mirror and back to the road, swerving to avoid wrapping Bessie around a stop sign.

"Don't try anything funny, especially you, Sam, as my orders are 'shoot to kill.'" Her voice was cold, leaving me with no doubt she would carry through with her threat.

Zanna hadn't said anything about not whimpering, so I started. Pitiful, high-pitched snivels, ramping up until I had myself in full-fledged hyperventilation, peppered with an occasional sneeze.

"Turn left here," my stowaway ordered. I held the steering wheel in a white-knuckled death grip, my gaze flicking between the road ahead and Zanna's reflection in my rearview mirror. She directed me through a cookie-cutter neighborhood of squatty brick ranches. "Turn at the blue mailbox," she barked.

I'm not sure how I missed the cerulean-blue mailbox that listed slightly at the curb, but I was half past it when Zanna whacked me on the back of the head. "Turn here, you stupid cow!"

I stopped the car, backed up, and made the turn. Zanna threw an automatic garage-door opener at Sam. "Open it."

Sam fumbled with the small gray box, finally getting her fingers to push the button. The garage door slid open. I drove in.

"Shut it," Zanna ordered. Sam pressed the button and the door rumbled back down, sealing us off from the rest of the world.

"That's Chief Bennett's truck," Sam whispered to me, jerking her head in the direction of a white compact pick-'em-up truck in the port next to us. Sam seemed to be taking this all in stride. I tried to draw some strength from her, but she didn't seem to be sharing.

"Yes, your friend is here, waiting for you to join him. Everyone out of the car, nice and easy now. Remember, at this point you're worth more to me dead than alive."

"Why not just shoot us and get it over with?"

I landed a hard elbow to Sam's ribs, and her breath whooshed out. What was she thinking, provoking Zanna like that? Maybe she didn't want to live to see another day, but I did.

"Because that Zucker bitch next door would have the cops all over my ass if she heard a gunshot. She calls if I so much as drop a can of beans on the floor. I need to get some packing done for my trip right now. The plan is for me to be out of the country long before they find your cold, decaying corpses."

She laughed like a crazy woman. What do I mean *like* one? She obviously *was* one.

A shiver racked my body and settled in my teeth, making them chatter like a pair of windup dentures.

"Are you and Chief Bennett disappearing together?" Sam asked as if we were making polite conversation at a garden party.

Zanna crazy-laughed again and poked me in the shoulder with the barrel of her gun. That was all the motivation I needed to scramble out of the car.

Zanna lined Sam and me up like kindergarteners heading

toward the lunchroom. I led the parade through the door leading from the garage, along a breezeway that looked like a
casualty of Hurricane Katrina, and into a kitchen that hadn't
been cleaned since the Clinton years. Even though Sam followed between Zanna's gun and me, it felt as if that cold metal
were pressed against the base of my skull.

"Chief Bennett is waiting for you in the basement." Zanna
stepped around me and tugged open a door that revealed a
stairway leading down into darkness.

I hesitated. Zanna pointed the gun at my forehead, and I
plunged forward. No need to ask me twice. With my right
hand on the rail and my left pressing against the plaster wall,
I stepped cautiously down the narrow steps. I heard Sam behind me. Small comfort, that. But it was better not to be alone
in circumstances like this.

The door slammed shut, extinguishing the little bit of light
we'd had, and I froze. The ominous click of a lock echoed in
the darkness. We were prisoners. In a place that reeked of cat
urine. I started to gag.

I heard Sam fumbling behind me, and it was only a matter of
seconds before the stairwell illuminated. One tiny bulb over our
heads gave off enough light to scare the mice into their holes
and cast shadows on the cobwebs. It also revealed one white,
fleshy arm poking out from under a blue plastic tarp at the
bottom of the steps.

I looked at Sam. She looked at me. And we both looked
down at the arm again. "Is that what I think it is?" I said, my
voice as shaky as my legs.

"Only one way to find out." Sam squeezed past me and down
the steps.

I didn't think Sam should be alone when she investigated.
Or maybe it was I who didn't want to be left alone cowering at
the top of the stairs when Zanna returned with her gun.
I caught up to Sam as she lifted the arm to check the pulse.
"Dead." She yanked off the tarp and we stared at the cold,
lifeless body of Chief Bennett. I'm no medical examiner, but
I guessed the single bullet hole to the temple is what killed

him. That or the blood loss—a huge puddle formed a halo behind his head.

I think I'd used up my lifetime supply of adrenaline by this time, as I felt nothing. No nausea. No revulsion. Not even a soupçon of fear. Even with those lifeless eyes staring at me, absolutely nothing. As if I were dead too. At least on the inside.

"I'd say he hasn't been dead that long," Sam said matter-of-factly. "No signs of rigor mortis yet. What did we learn from our research? It takes about three to ten hours to set in. Plus his hands are still warm. Here, feel it."

I did. I bent down and wrapped my hand around his. Not 98.6 degree warmth, but still warmer than this dank cellar. Yup, he was freshly dead all right. And that would be my fate too, if Sam and I didn't figure out a way to save ourselves. "How long do you think it will be before Zanna comes back to kill us?"

Sam shrugged. "It's not like she needs only enough for a two-week vacation. She's leaving and never coming back."

"So, maybe thirty minutes?"

"Maybe. Why?"

"The only thing we have on our side right now is the element of surprise. I think we can take her, especially if it's dark down here."

"But she has a gun," Sam said.

I wish she hadn't reminded me. "I know, I know. But we're going to have to take our chances."

"What do you propose?"

I looked around the empty, windowless basement. No discarded furniture, no boxes of Christmas decorations, no way of escape or anything that could be used as a weapon.

Second option would be calling in the cavalry. But my cell phone was tucked safely away in Bessie's console.

Third, and the only workable option, seemed to be overpowering our captor. But that was very risky, considering she had a gun.

"If I put you on my shoulders, I think you'll be able to reach the lightbulb to unscrew it. Darkness can be used to our advantage."

Sam nodded.

"Then we'll tuck ourselves back under the stairs here, and when she comes down looking for us, we'll tackle her. I'll hit her low and knock her over. You go for the arm and the gun."

Sam seemed to be weighing her odds of survival.

"Do you have a better idea?" I asked.

Sam's mouth set in a determined grin. "I think we can do this." We knuckle tapped, then hugged. Teamwork.

Sam wasn't as light as she looked, or I wasn't as strong as I thought, and getting her onto my shoulders while I stood on a step halfway down the staircase was not going to happen.

"Come on, Ellery. Dig deep. Use those glutes for the reason God intended. Come on. You can do it." Sam's inner cheerleader came out.

I channeled the energy I would have used to shut her up, and slowly we rose toward the light fixture. I braced my legs shoulder-width apart, and I felt like an Olympic clean-and-jerk weightlifter when they held the barbells over their head.

"Hurry up!" I hissed, not sure how much longer I'd be able to hold her.

"It's hot. Wait."

But I couldn't. Her hand on my forehead tipped my head backward just enough that I lost my balance and we plunged backward down half a dozen steps.

But amid a tinkle and shower of broken glass, the light had been extinguished.

"Are you okay?"

"I think I cut my hand on the lightbulb."

I shifted my weight, crunching glass under my foot as I checked for broken bones and lumps on my head. "Sorry about that."

"All's well that ends well. We achieved our goal. We're in the dark."

"Do you think Zanna heard us?"

"How could she not? It sounded like a semi smashing through her house."

We waited, not daring even to breathe, listening for the sound of the key turning in the lock. A nervous giggle bubbled forth from me. "This has to be a dream. No, a nightmare. I'm going to wake up any moment."

Sam started laughing too. "Wait until I tell George! I've been complaining that our lives are boring—"

More giggles.

"We'd better hide. Zanna could be here any minute."

We crawled around and tucked ourselves under the staircase. Spiderwebs clung to my hair and arms, but I left them there. A mouse ran across my hand, but I didn't scream. Chief Bennett's knee touched mine, but I didn't move, because I knew if I did, we'd end up just like him.

"I've changed my mind," Sam whispered.

"A little late for that, don't you think?" I hissed back.

"No, I mean about the killer. I think it's Zanna. Not Lorraine."

"Gee, what was your first clue?"

"Now, El, let's not get churlish."

I sighed.

"I can't figure out why Chief Bennett is dead, though. How he figured into this. Maybe he found out about the skimming and was blackmailing about that too." Sam remained silent for a few moments. "Some detectives we turned out to be. I figured with our names, we'd be naturals."

"What?"

"You know, Ellery and Sam, as in Ellery Queen and Sam Spade. Two very famous detectives."

"Fictional detectives."

"Still."

I sighed again. "I never should have let you talk me into this."

"I didn't think it would be so dangerous."

At the sound of footsteps above us, we both hushed. I strained my ears and heard the faint click of a key in the lock.

"Showtime," I whispered and tensed my muscles, prepared to pounce.

Chapter Twenty-nine

My heart pounded so loudly I swore it would give away our hiding place. I felt sure Zanna could hear it as she crept down the steps above us. The dried wood squeaked with every step. Squeak. Pause. Squeak. Pause. Forget the Chinese water torture. Listening to your killer's footsteps as she stalked you was beyond cruel.

"I know you're down here," Zanna called. "Did you find your friend?" Squeak. Pause. "Chief Bennett had a big mouth and needed to be silenced." Squeak. Pause. "And you need to be silenced too, because he told me how much he'd told you. We can't have Twiddy's past come back to haunt us now, can we?" Squeak. Squeak. Scratch. She'd hit the dirt floor.

I dared not speak. Not yet. I just waited until the right moment. I reached out through the darkness and found Sam's hand. It was colder than Chief Bennett's. She gave me a reassuring squeeze, and I squeezed back, as if to say, "We're in this together." I don't think I would be anywhere near this calm were I alone. At least not without benefit of an elephant's dosage of Xanax.

"Why don't you save us all some trouble and come out where I can see you?"

So far our plan was working. The small triangle of light that came through the door did not illuminate the darkest recesses of the basement. A scratching noise came from the far corner of the room, a mouse, no doubt. The crack of gunfire split the air. "Now!" Sam yelled.

I stood up too quickly, bumped my head on the bottom of the stairs, and tripped forward, landing across Chief Bennett's dead body and two feet short of my target. Sam's foot landed in the middle of my back as she climbed over me. Only she didn't go for Zanna. Or the gun. Sam went for the door. Straight up the stairs like a frightened jackrabbit, leaving me staring up at the nozzle of Zanna's gun.

"Nice and slow, now. I need to get you out of here before the cops show up. You can be my hostage, my ticket to freedom. Nobody would dare put the life of Braddocks Beach's genetic royalty in jeopardy." She sniggered. An evil snigger that set my arm and neck hairs at attention.

In all my forty-eight years on Earth, I'd never seen a gun up close and personal, especially one locked, loaded, and pointed at my face. It vibrated back and forth like a hummingbird on speed.

In a moment of pre-death clarity, I realized Zanna's hand was as steady as a rock; it was my head that was quivering. The rest of my body followed suit.

I rose slowly, put my hands in the air the way they do on TV, and preceded my anticipated killer up the steps. I wondered for a second if I was already dead, for I seemed to be having some sort of out-of-body experience, watching the scene unfold, but not being part of it.

"Outside," Zanna ordered. "Get in my car. Quick. I've got my gun pointed at your back, and if you so much as twist your head one centimeter to either side, I'll shoot. I've got three bullets left, and they all have your name on them."

The screen door squeaked as I led my way out into the sunshine. Out of the corner of my eye, I caught an image of Pip-squeak lifting his leg against Zanna's blue mailbox. What I wouldn't give to have half of a hamburger in my pocket right now. Wait. I didn't have a hamburger—

But I did have some pâté.

It was a mere wisp of an idea that quickly spun itself into a full-fledged plan.

I started sneezing. I really was allergic to Zanna. Maybe it was her scent of evil.

I reached my hand into my pocket, hoping Zanna would

perceive it as a natural reaction to reach for a Kleenex, and wrapped my fingers around a glob of Veralee's oozing goose liver. In one graceful karate move, I spun myself around, arm extended, and swatted Zanna across the face, leaving a trail of baby-food-brown ooze down her cheek.

Pipsqueak's nose didn't fail me. He flew through the air and was on her face like melted chocolate on a vinyl car seat in the summer. Zanna stumbled backward, using both hands to swat Pipsqueak away. As I'd hoped, that little mongrel wasn't going to stop until every morsel of goose liver was in his stomach.

I spotted the gun lying by Zanna's knee.

The next thing I knew, the gun was in my hand and pointed at her head.

She lunged at me.

I pulled the trigger.

Somebody screamed, "I've been shot! I've been shot!"

That's when all hell broke loose.

All seven members of the Braddocks Beach police force arrived en masse. They piled out of their sedans and raced in my direction. Sam, bless her busybody soul, led the charge. "Are you okay?" she asked.

I'd never been so glad to see that little sparkplug in my life. I felt a tear trickle down my cheek. "Is it over?"

"Yes, El. It's all over."

I collapsed to the asphalt, flat on my back, spread-eagled, rejoicing in every poke of a pebble under me that assured me I was alive. I turned my head and through my tears watched the drama play out before me.

I'd missed Zanna when I'd fired the gun. The police hauled her off in handcuffs. She cussed up a storm about suing them for false arrest.

The paramedics treated Mrs. Zucker for a flesh wound to her arm and carried her to the hospital on account of her age. My shot had gone so wild it had hit the unlucky woman on the other side of the hedge. I hadn't even seen her.

Officer Compton made me promise never to handle a gun

again until I'd taken some lessons. Not a problem. I had no desire to be on either side of a gun for the rest of my life.

Somehow, I ended up with custody of Pipsqueak, at least for the night. Mrs. Zucker insisted I was the only one who would take good care of her little snookums. What could I say? This little bundle of white fur had just saved my life. It was the least I could do.

We waited and watched while they wheeled Chief Bennett's body out from the basement.

Officer Compton took our statements, the little bit that we knew at that point, and promised we'd be the first to know when they filled in the missing pieces.

Still so many questions, so many loose ends. But the physical, mental, emotional, and spiritual exhaustion that filled every cell in my body took priority.

"Food or sleep first?" Sam asked as I backed Bessie down Zanna's driveway.

"Sleep." I was too tired to eat.

There's always a first time for everything.

Chapter Thirty

Sirens and screams tugged at the edge of my sleep. I pulled my pillow over my head. Not so easy to ignore was the incessant shaking that made my molars rattle. "What?" I yelled into my pillow.

"Ellery! Ellery!"

I hated dreams like this, ones that seemed so real you almost woke up.

"Ellery, wake up. We have an emergency."

"I'm sleeping."

Silence replaced the sirens.

Bright light replaced the darkness.

Freezing water replaced my warm pillow.

A strange voice reverberated in my ear. "Ellery. Sorry I had to do that, but you wouldn't wake up. You need to get dressed. Quickly."

I shook the sleep from my brain and wiped the water from my face.

"Come on, now. We're meeting Mystic in thirty minutes."

"Huh?" I forced my eyes open, blinking against the bright sunshine streaming through the window, but confused as to where I was.

"Breakfast at Tinky's," Sam said.

That was all I needed to hear to get me up. Every muscle in my body screamed in protest as I rolled my feet to the floor and my torso to a sitting position. I racked my brain trying to remember if I'd been run over by a Mack truck.

No, but we had chased down a killer. We'd solved a murder. Two murders. Three murders, if you include Chief Bennett's.

Not so much solved them, but stumbled and bumbled our way along and in the process flushed out the killers. Pure dumb luck.

"What time is it?"

"Seven."

I did the math. I'd been asleep for sixteen hours. Still six hours short of my weekend quota. How many meals had ɪ missed? My stomach sounded like a roaring lion when I started to count. "Can't we wait until nine?"

"No, Mystic's meeting us. I promised her an exclusive in exchange for her sharing all she's learned while we slept. Twiddy was arrested and spilled his guts, I guess."

Sam herded me into the bathroom and laid black dress pants and a lightweight white sweater across the vanity, then disappeared while I showered and dressed. With the promise of Tinky's omelet, I was very efficient and soon joined Sam downstairs.

Sam looked amazing, considering she'd been through even more than I had the past few days. She must have used an entire tube of extra-strength concealer to cover up the bruise on her temple. If I looked real close, I could see a little bit of green at the corner of her eye. But other than that, she looked fantastic. Not a hair was out of place, gelled into cascading blond curls. She looked smart in a ruby-red sundress and flat, bejeweled flip-flops. A strand of pearls added class to an already classy lady. I doubt under normal circumstances we would have ever become friends. We came from different worlds. But our recent tribulations formed a bond that would keep us together for a long time.

"You might want to think about a little liposuction around those jowls."

I sighed. She was only trying to help.

We walked, side by side, to Tinky's. The chickadee's melody had never sounded so sweet. The sky had never seemed so blue. The trees never so green. The peonies so bountiful. The air so fresh. Facing death seemed to have made me appreciate life a little bit more.

"Officer Compton told me they caught Twiddy driving west in a rental car."

"I'm sorry," I said, laying a hand on Sam's arm. "I know he was a friend of yours."

"He had us all hoodwinked. When confronted, he admitted to killing that Jezebel back in college and skimming money from the town's coffers, almost two million dollars over the past twenty years, to pay the blackmail money to Bennett. They could have taken us for another million with no one the wiser. It was your call to the SBI that launched the investigation into Connie's death. Chief Bennett realized the jig was up and tried to run."

"So we can take all the credit for flushing them out."

Sam smiled and nodded. I held out my fist and Sam knuckle-tapped me.

"Did he also confess to Connie's murder?"

"Yup, he did. As Bennett said, Viagra in the chicken salad. Connie has never passed up Scootch's homemade chicken salad, so Twiddy knew he would ingest a goodly amount, hopefully mistaking the crunchiness for fresh pecans. Death wasn't a certainty, but if it didn't work, they had a more sure-fire way that involved cement shoes and Lake Braddock. Only Connie wasn't killed for the reason we thought. It turns out that you were correct. Cordy was Twiddy's biological daughter, the result of an on-again, off-again affair that he and Lorraine had been having for the past twenty-five years. Can you believe they managed to keep it a secret for that long?"

Knowing the little bit that I did about this close-knit community, that did seem unbelievable.

"He'd been blackmailing Lorraine too. Threatening to go to Connie about the truth. Twiddy was a greedy little booger, wasn't he?"

Greedy booger was much too mild a term. But Sam didn't strike me as the type who would utter a cussword, no matter how fitting.

"Lorraine knew if Connie found out, a divorce would ensue,

and there would go her place among Braddocks Beach's social elite. Not to mention that Cordy might lose out on her inheritance, although I doubt it, because Connie loved that girl like she was his own. I don't think he would have done that to her. Lorraine, well, we know he'd already set those wheels in motion to leave her penniless." A Cheshire Cat–like grin spread across Sam's face.

"So there's no problem with Cordy and Fitz-Two getting married now?"

"None whatsoever. Although I did hear through the BBG, that's the Braddocks Beach Grapevine, that the ceremony would be postponed at least six months, what with Connie's death and all."

"Christmas weddings are nice."

"Yes, they are." We strolled in companionable silence for half a block. "I guess we had the motive wrong. It wasn't that somebody didn't want it to be discovered that Cordy and Fitz-Two were first cousins. It's that Twiddy didn't want anyone to find out they *weren't* first cousins. Then his blackmailing of Lorraine would come to an end. He's the one who snatched the DNA letter. He and Zanna had been visiting Lorraine and came over to see what all the commotion was about."

"I didn't see him in all the confusion. Was it Chief Bennett who shot at us at the church?"

"No, Zanna confessed to that. She had just killed Bennett in her basement and was taking his truck back to his cabin when she spotted us. Twiddy was following, but I guess we didn't see him. Lily-livered chicken poop that he was, he ran as soon as he saw Zanna open fire. They didn't catch up with him until Dayton." Sam held the door to Tinky's open for me and motioned for me to precede her inside. The smell knocked my socks off. Sizzling bacon, aromatic muffins, and coffee. Strong, black, strip-the-paint-from-your-car coffee.

We joined Mystic in a booth at the back corner of the café, where she was already tucking into a bowl of white biscuits nestled in a sea of sausage gravy. It took every ounce of self-control for me to not grab my fork and snatch a few bites off Mystic's plate, but I'm quite certain Sam would let me know that Queen Bees didn't eat off others' plates.

Mystic set her tape recorder on the table. "So let's start at the beginning. Who killed Isabel Tinsdale?"

"Twiddy and Zanna are pointing the finger at Chief Bennett," Sam answered. "I'm not sure if that's because he really did it, or because he isn't around to defend himself."

"Did they give a motive?" Mystic asked.

"Zanna said Mizizzy had taken a midnight stroll to the lighthouse; she'd been having trouble sleeping. Maybe all the dirt she and Connie had been digging up about BB residents weighed heavily on her mind. Anyway, she'd overheard Chief Bennett shaking down Twiddy for more money because he'd somehow found out about their skimming of the books. Twiddy knew the jig would be up if their scam was uncovered. Chief Bennett panicked when he heard Mizizzy in the crow's nest."

"Do you believe them?"

"I don't know. It could have been either Twiddy or Zanna herself for the same reason—overhearing something."

An image of Chief Bennett "welcoming" me to Braddocks Beach popped into my head. So cocky, the way his hand slid to his gun. His left hand. Epiphany. "Bennett killed Aunt Izzy."

"How do you know?" Mystic asked, forking another bite of gravy-laden biscuit into her mouth.

"Because we'd learned Aunt Izzy had the right side of her face smashed in. From the front, I was told. In order for that to happen, it would take a left-handed swing, don't you think?" I clasped my hands together and assumed a bent-elbowed, left-handed baseball swing-for-the-bleachers movement. "Chief Bennett was the only one of the three who was left-handed. Besides, it makes sense that he treated it as an accident instead of a murder so that evidence could be contaminated. Probably had nothing to do with not wanting crime-scene tape in the tourist district."

"Good job, Ellery Queen," Sam said.

"Thank you, Sam Spade."

We double knuckle-tapped.

The waitress arrived with our plates of food, a western omelet, real home fries with chunks of potatoes and wedges of Vidalia onions, and a side of pancakes with butter pecan syrup for me. Sam's bran muffin looked lonely sitting in the middle of her plate.

I lifted my fork just as Mystic's cell phone started to play "Margaritaville." She snapped it open and lifted it to her ear. "Sayers. Speak."

Mystic's face paled as she started gathering her belongings. "Got it," she said into the phone, then to us, "Sorry to run. There's breaking news over on Charleston Avenue."

"What's up?" Sam asked as she took her first bite of muffin.

"They just found Lorraine Littleton lying in a pool of blood."

Chapter Thirty-one

Mystic and Sam raced out of the restaurant, with the little leprechaun body slamming the newspaper reporter out of the way as they battled to be the first out the door.

I followed at a slightly more dignified pace, but shoving a rolled-up pancake into my mouth as I went probably negated any appearance of decorum. Like they say, you can't make a Queen Bee out of a sow's ear.

Mystic's black Excursion was pulling away from the curb as I approached. I jumped onto the running board, grabbed the luggage rack, and held on for all I was worth. Riding commando was an experience I hoped never to repeat, as the g-forces that pull and push you when swerving around corners drain the blood from your head. How did firemen hang on the backs of those hook-and-ladder trucks?

But I arrived in one piece. And, not having to bother with unfastening a seat belt or fumbling with opening the door, I was the first on the scene.

Cordy sat at the top of the steps of her family home, her arms tucked across her midsection, staring at the heap of human lying on the sidewalk.

As I got closer, I did see a pool of blood. Well, more like a puddle. That might be stretching it. I'd call it a few drops, and Lorraine lying with her head right next to it. She had a gash at her temple that hadn't coagulated yet.

I heard Sam and Mystic skitter to a stop behind me just as Lorraine broke out in a chorus of "Noooooobody knooooo-wwws the troublllle I've seeeeeen."

"Drunk?" Sam asked.

"As a skunk," Cordy answered.

"Kind of early in the day for that, isn't it?"

"It started last night, when Max stopped by and gave her the news."

Sam and I looked at each other and grimaced. Poor Lorraine.

Mystic pulled her tape recorder from her pocket and shoved it in Cordy's face. "What news?"

"Family business." Cordy dismissed her with a turn of her head.

"Noooooobody knoooooows but Jesuuuuuussssssss," Lorraine crooned.

"Should we get her inside?"

Cordy nodded and rose from the steps.

We got Lorraine to her feet, me on one side (the side without the blood) and Sam on the other, and half dragged, half frog-marched her up the steps.

"Noooooobody knoooooows, the troubllllle I've seeeeen. Glory halleluuuuuuuuuuuuuuuuujah."

Cordy shut the door in Mystic's face while Sam and I settled Lorraine in the downstairs bathroom, resting her head on a fluffy white towel.

"Think she'll be okay?" Sam asked as we settled into chairs in the kitchen.

"I thought I knew my dad. Why would he do this to her?" Cordy's voice cracked and she wiped a tear from her eye.

"If there's one thing I've learned over the past forty-eight hours, it's that we only know things about a person that they want us to know. I think both your parents were trying to protect you." Sam laid a hand on Cordy's arm.

Cordy sniffled and nodded. "To think Mom was in Twiddy's arms while Dad lay dying." Cordy's face scrunched up as if she had a mouthful of Sour Patch Kids. "It sickens me to think that that man's genes run through my veins." She shook off the image.

I shuddered too.

A young, dark-haired man sporting a nine o'clock shadow

burst through the back door. He ran to Cordy's side. She raced to his arms and dissolved into hysterical sobs. I heard mumbled terms of endearment and soothing predictions of the future and concluded that this must be her one and only. And not her long-lost first cousin. They made a darling couple.

Sam touched me on the arm and nodded for us to leave. "Funny, isn't it?"

"What's funny about it? These last few days shaved years off my life."

"Not ha-ha funny, but ironic funny that the mayor's receptionist's version of what happened was so close to the truth. Blackmail. Jealousy. Romantic entanglements. So many lives destroyed over it all. But if I were to look for a silver lining," Sam waxed poetic as we crossed Charleston Avenue, "it's that it brought us together. We make quite a team, you and I."

Tears turned Sam's eyes a sparkling emerald green. She held out her hand for one of our teamwork knuckle taps. Instead, I pulled her into my arms and hugged her tight. She hugged me back in heartfelt friendship.

"I know it's not my place to tell you what to do, but I'd be very happy to call you my neighbor."

My strengthened hug was my answer. I'd come to appreciate all Braddocks Beach had to offer in the way of small-town living. Its strong sense of community and lifelong friendships. I think at that moment I made a conscious decision to stay. Maybe they published a *Queen Bees for Dummies* manual that would help me ease into my new role.

But it's still the lazy, hazy, crazy days of summer. I might change my mind when the first snowflake falls. I'd keep my options open for a while.

"How about I rustle us up some breakfast?" Sam offered when we stepped away from each other.

"You don't have to ask me twice." I smiled and motioned for her to lead the way. She hooked her arm through mine as we stepped through the lilac hedge toward her backyard.

"I was just thinking," Sam said in her usual fast pace. "There's a lot of mystery surrounding the way your father left town. Maybe we could ask a few questions, interview some of the older citizens."

"Nope," I said in a voice that brooked no argument. "I'm hanging up my detective shoes before someone—me—gets hurt."

"What danger is there in asking a few questions? It's not like your dad was murdered and we're chasing down a killer. Just a simple puzzle. We'll ask a few questions. Somebody has to know something. Don't you want to know the truth?"

Of course I did. And when I became rich, I'd hire someone to find out what happened.